# Larkin

## ON THE SHORE

### A NOVEL

# JEAN MILLS

## Larkin

## ON THE SHORE

### A NOVEL

Red Deer Press

Copyright © 2019 Jean Mills

Published in the United States in 2020

Published in Canada by Red Deer Press,
195 Allstate Parkway, Markham, ON   L3R 4T8

Published in the United States by Red Deer Press,
311 Washington Street, Brighton, MA  02135

**Library and Archives Canada Cataloguing in Publication**

Title: Larkin on the shore / by Jean Mills.
Names: Mills, Jean, 1955- author.
Identifiers: Canadiana 20190156074 | ISBN 9780889955776 (softcover)
Classification: LCC PS8576.I5654 L37 2019 | DDC jC813/.54—dc23

**Publisher Cataloging-in-Publication Data (U.S.**

Names: Mills, Jean, 1955-, author.
Title:  Larkin on the Shore / Jean Mills.
Description: Markham, Ontario : Fitzhenry and Whiteside, 2019. | Summary: "This beautifully crafted
coming-of-age young adult novel set in Nova Scotia focuses on a young woman's family, friendships,
conflicts, healing and inner-strength"-- Provided by publisher.
Identifiers: ISBN 978-0-88995-577-6 (paperback)
Subjects: LCSH:  Nova Scotia – Fiction. | Adulthood – Fiction. | Detective and mystery fiction. |
Bildungsromans. | BISAC: YOUNG ADULT FICTION / Law & Crime.
Classification: LCC PZ7.M555La | DDC 813.6 – dc23

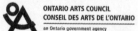

**ONTARIO ARTS COUNCIL**
**CONSEIL DES ARTS DE L'ONTARIO**
an Ontario government agency
un organisme du gouvernement de l'Ontario

Canada Council   Conseil des arts
for the Arts      du Canada

Red Deer Press acknowledges with thanks the Canada Council for the Arts and the Ontario Arts Council
for their support of our publishing program.  We acknowledge the financial support of the Government of
Canada through the Canada Book Fund (CBF) for our publishing activities.

2 4 6 8 10 9 7 5 3 1

Edited for the Press by Peter Carver
Text and cover design by Tanya Montini
Printed in Canada by Houghton Boston

www.reddeerpress.com

For my Mills, Rice, and Clark families,
who love the shore as much as I do.

# Sunset, Day 1

It would be so easy, just walking out across the sandbars and never stopping until I'm in over my head.

Maybe right now, at sunset. At least now I have a target to aim for when I hit the slimy rocks and seaweed. And the crabs. And those little shrimpy things that went all attack mode on my feet in the tidal pools earlier this afternoon. The last thing I'll see is the blinding reflection of the setting sun on the water, before the green flash shoots up (something I've never seen, but Dad swears is for real). Because I'd close my eyes, of course, as soon as the water reaches my nose. Close my eyes, take a deep breath, keep walking, walking. Drift away.

Okay, it's salt water, so I'd probably float a bit, which would be inconvenient. But if I kept my running shoes on I wouldn't feel the slimy stuff then, and my shoes would fill with water and keep me anchored to the sand and rocks and seaweed—right?

That's it. Just walk over the sandbars. Keep going. Go deep. Never come up.

It would be so much easier than this.

# Emergency room

I don't remember everything about that night, but I do remember bits.

Like, Dad carrying me from the dark car into the hospital and how bright it is.

I remember Lynette doing the driving because Dad's arms are wrapped around me as he holds me close in the back seat. He's shaking and I'm probably shaking, too, but mostly I just feel sick.

Their voices, but I have no idea what they're saying to each other.

Then him sliding awkwardly out of the car, carrying me because I can't walk. Because I'm gone again, everything black.

Voices. I lie on the bed, or table, or whatever, and someone shines lights in my eyes and feels up and down my arms and legs.

"Larkin, can you move your arms? Good girl. Fingers? Great, Larkin. How about your feet? Good girl."

I can feel everything. And it all hurts.

I want to say something, but I just can't find the words to tell them not to let Jonah in. I try but they shush me.

"It's okay, Larkin. Just breathe, Larkin."

Time passes. More poking. Hands feeling my stomach and below that, feeling my head, my jaw, my nose, which hurts.

Someone says, "Alcohol, drugs for sure." Maybe me.

And then I'm able to say, "I'm going to be sick," and hands help me sit up to the side and puke into a metal container where it all splashes around. The pain in my head makes me cry. And I just puke some more.

Lie down. Don't hear anything for a while.

Dad's on the other side of a blue curtain, talking to someone.

"Her friends brought her home. Said she fell out of a moving car and hit her head. Car just drove off. Left her there and drove off. Just drove off …"

My dad's voice doesn't sound like his voice at all. Maybe it's not him? Maybe I'm dreaming?

"Rape kit," someone says, and I try to say something then, but everything is dark and getting darker.

"He didn't rape me. Well, maybe he tried, but I didn't let

him." That's what I want to say but I'm so not sure of anything now. Not even sure what happened. The party, the drinks, the joints, the other stuff, Jonah's hands and breath, and then his dark car, and thinking, *Here? Now? Is this going to be it?* And him laughing at me, and then we're fighting, and an explosion in my head as something hits me … Was it his hand? The hard pavement? Then nausea and darkness. Amanda's face, all scared, and hands helping me up, into somebody's car, but not Jonah's. And suddenly a spotlight. No, the door opening and someone flicking on the outside light as I lie there on the front porch with Amanda crouched beside me.

My dad, finding me like that. My dad, crying in the car as he holds me in his arms all the way to the hospital.

I want to forget. I want to forget everything.

# My face in the mirror

I'm caught by surprise when I look in the mirror in the washroom at Pearson. Lately I've been avoiding mirrors, but I have to wash my hands, try to avoid the germs people spew around airports. So I soap up, rub and rinse, look up, and see myself looking back.

The periorbital hematoma is fading to green. Dad said it would change colors, and it has. Dark purple, then lilac, green, yellow. The bruise on my jaw is greenish now. The one on my arm fading to yellow. But that black eye is taking its time.

Thank goodness for the concealer Lynette gave me. She's not great, overall, but she sure knows her makeup.

And it helps, because once I board AC4874 to Moncton, the other passengers don't seem to notice the girl in Row 17, Seat A, by the window. I'm hunched inside my hoodie, sleeves pulled down, hair loose and hanging forward, earbuds in.

Invisible.

# Granne

My grandmother meets me at the airport in Moncton.

Grandma Anne. Also and always known to me as Granne. (Get it?) My father's mother, which is difficult to believe, actually, because he's so soft and she's so hard.

Not hard, exactly. And not soft exactly, either. But she's firm, I think you could say. And my father is not firm. Not around me, anyway.

"Larkin." That's all she says as she steps toward me in the Arrivals hall at the Moncton airport for an awkward hug. "You're here. And in one piece, too."

"Hi, Granne." I'm not sure what she means with that last part. Or maybe I do. She's been talking to my father, of course. And then there's that green and purple tinge around my left eye that even Lynette's concealer can't completely conceal.

"Your bags will be over here."

I follow her toward the baggage carousel. People all around us are hugging and talking, the usual airport scene.

"Good flight?" she asks and I nod. She has a teacher voice. A principal voice, actually. She's retired now, but I can just imagine her up front at morning assembly, making the announcements about timetable changes or rule infractions. *And to the person who wrote that inappropriate message on the mirror in the second floor boys washroom, rest assured, I will be speaking with you today.* Or at grad, handing out diplomas and telling the parents how wonderful their children are.

"I'm supposed to send Dad a selfie so he knows I got here," I say and hope she's not going to go all *oh-you-kids-and-your-phones* on me. Or ask why he thinks I might not have got here. She doesn't.

"Good idea." She nods. Moves into position beside me as I line us up in my phone's camera.

Our two faces fill the screen, neither of us smiling. Just watching ourselves, more like we're looking through a window. I feel her hand, just a whisper of pressure, on my shoulder as I click. She steps away.

"How awful is it?" she asks, so I show her. "Yup. Pretty awful."

14

And then she snorts a laugh. "Well, my side of it, anyway."

I think I probably win the "pretty awful" prize, but I just smile to let her know I heard her little joke before I get down to texting the photo to my dad.

Here in Moncton

He responds within seconds.

Thanks. Say hi to Granne. Flight just called. Will text from Vancouver.

No texting mushiness from my dad. No XOXOXO or hugs or emoticons.

We said goodbye at Pearson this morning at my departure gate. His flight was hours later than mine, but he came with me anyway. Planned to buy his way into the Maple Leaf Lounge and hang out with all the snacks and uninterrupted reading time. He's currently working his way through some Scottish detective series. Escapist no-brainer reading, he calls it. A change from teaching Shakespeare and poetry and CanLit novels during the school year.

Yes, I'm surrounded by teachers.

"Try to have fun," he says as he wraps his arms around me

at the gate. My flight has been called and almost everyone has boarded now, and my heart has suddenly started to beat really fast and I'm having trouble swallowing. My arms around his waist. I have a flashback of him swinging me high in the air, over his head. Us laughing, laughing. Sunshine and waves and wind.

"I will," I manage. Say it into his shoulder so he probably doesn't hear.

"We're going to be okay, Lark," he whispers close to my ear.

Hours ago. Feels like months.

I text him back. Want to say more but settle for:

K love you

I don't tell him to try and have fun.

A buzzer sounds and the baggage carousel squeaks into action. The first bags bounce down onto the belt and people edge forward, establishing their position, ready to pounce.

Granne and I just stay where we are. I can see the bags dropping out of the chute and I'll go get mine when it appears. I hate being jostled. Granne is just standing there beside me, waiting. Maybe we have this in common.

Hard to say what else we have in common. I haven't seen

her for six years, since I was ten, the first summer without my mother. The weather was spectacular that year—days of skin-searing sun, and so windy that we didn't feel its heat (until later, when Granne had to slather me in cold aloe gel that she keeps in the fridge), and red sand on everything, everywhere, even around my toenails. It was there for days, even after I got home, many baths later.

I think that year my dad was trying to drown me in summer so I wouldn't notice that anything was wrong. Granne supplied jam and biscuits, and fat sweet cinnamon rolls. And tea—stronger than my mother ever made it, and black, not pale and smelling of flowers. Lemonade. Coke. My first Coke. They talked about books and Granne asked me what I was reading (some mystery series that everyone at school was into), and she took me to the library in the village, housed in the old train station. I slept so well there at Granne's house. Waves sighed over the sandbars all night like a lullaby. Tide in, tide out. Every morning the shore looked different. Granne and I walked up and down the sand for hours looking for sea glass, shells, colored stones. We talked. I don't remember a word we said.

Now I'm standing beside her in the Moncton airport, waiting

for my suitcase to make its appearance and bump around the belt to where we wait.

"There it is," I say, moving forward as my large maroon case plops onto the belt.

"Good," she says.

I have no idea what we're going to talk about for the next two months.

# Piper

Granne and I stop in Sackville at the Timmy's drive-thru for a late lunch for me, a coffee for each of us. Then back on the highway. Conversation is sparse because, well, we have the whole summer, and there's really not much to say at this point, is there?

"Do you want to see if the piper's playing?" she asks as we cross the border into Nova Scotia and the sign for the tourist information center flashes by.

A memory—my dad: "Do you want to see if the piper's playing?" and I had no idea what this meant. But he seemed so eager to show me that I shrugged and nodded *okay*, and we drove through the parking lot, full of buses of Japanese tourists and families with kids and dogs, our windows down, listening for the piper. Gulls, kids calling out, car engines humming, trucks on the highway. No piper.

"Must be his break," said Dad.

He seemed way more disappointed than I was. Hard to be disappointed about missing something you didn't know was there in the first place.

"What does the piper do?"

"You know, bagpipes. Kilt. The whole welcome to Nova Scotia Scottish thing."

"Oh."

I was ten. What did I know? This was the first trip I remember to visit Granne at her house, Dad's old house. Where he grew up. We'd come once when I was a baby, but now I'm so confused about Mom and everything, I don't even ask why we've never come back since then. The only time I'd seen Granne was when she came to visit us in Toronto, staying in a hotel because she said fish and visitors stink after three days. She took me to the ROM, and out for a shopping trip at the Eaton Centre. The Science Centre. She came for supper a few times, although my mother turned into her other self—her tight, nervous self—when Granne was there, I don't know why. Maybe Granne knows about Mom and the pills and stuff. And Mom knows that Granne knows. I was little. I was in a haze of confused kid-dom. I just knew that

Granne and my mother didn't like each other. Or something. Granne and Dad and I took the ferry to the Toronto Island and rented bikes. Seeing Granne riding a bike was like watching Mary Poppins, all upright and steady and no wobbling.

She came again in winter and she took me to the ballet. *The Nutcracker*, so it must have been Christmas time. Hazy. I don't remember much about it.

"Larkin?"

"Oh, sorry. No, it's okay."

"Well, we're going past it anyway. If you roll down your window and the pipes are going, you might be able to hear."

I obediently roll down my window. The ramp off the highway leads up past the tourist center. I look over, listen. Same remembered cars, buses, flags, faint voices, a dog barking.

But no piper.

# Wildlife on the shore

After a late supper of lobster chowder and biscuits, homemade by Granne—"one of my specialties," she says, "in honor of your arrival"—we sit on the back deck, watching the tide come in and the sun go down. She's working on a glass of white wine. No, she doesn't offer me one.

The water—the ocean, I guess, or this little corner of it known as the Northumberland Strait—freaks me out a bit. Not the water, exactly, but the life that lives in and under it. The creepy little shrimp that attacked my bare feet as we walked in the tidal pools before supper. The waving seaweed that lies slick and slimy on the red rocks and just under the surface at the tide line. Moving. As if it's alive. (Well, of course it's alive, but like it's thinking and moving on its own.) The stones that seem to roll over and bite the bottom of my soft, city, shoes-only feet.

This all feels way different from that visit when I was ten.

So, after supper and clean-up, and some random unpacking and lying on my bed, staring at the ceiling to kill time, it's me and Granne and her wine. The deck. The tide coming in. I'm full of chowder and biscuits, and dreaming of bedtime, of pulling the blankets up over my head.

"Best place to watch the sunset is from the beach," she says. Takes a sip. "You should go down."

Is she trying to get rid of me? Maybe she wants to light up and doesn't want me to see. Or probably she thinks it's dangerous for me to be anywhere near her wine. I don't know what Dad has told her about the whole periorbital hematoma thing.

"Sure. Okay." Path of least resistance. That's what Dad calls it. Just go with the flow. It doesn't always work out but, come on, what trouble can I get into on the beach with her lifeguarding me from up here?

"There's an old quilt in the mud room," she says. "Take that to sit on. You'll feel cozier."

"Sure. Okay."

I notice she doesn't offer to join me.

The ancient quilt is surprisingly heavy, with the puffy filling all lumpy in some spots and completely missing in others, so that the two sides (one looks like squares cut from old pajamas, the other pale, stained, and yellowing, like some old sheet, maybe) stick together. I imagine years of salt water and damp sand soaking into the fabric. Charming.

I lug it down across the yard to the path that leads between the rocks onto the shore and start walking. Don't have to turn around and look back up at the house to know she's watching me.

So I go down the beach, marching along as if I mean it, toward the point. Pick a spot way down, a sort of sandy alcove marked by tall grass and beachy-type white wildflowers. Spread the quilt and plop down on it. Then look.

Yup. She's still there. Still sipping.

The sun is getting lower, getting bigger and redder, all dramatic. Pretty spectacular, actually.

But it's the water creeping up over the sandbars that really draws me. Because I can't stop thinking about walking out there, walking over the sand, through the pools, until I reach the last sandbar before the deeps.

It would be so easy, just walking out across the sandbars and never stopping until I'm in over my head.

Glance up. Yup, still there. Is she even watching me?

The sun has exploded into the few streaky clouds over the horizon now. Yellow, pink, red, purple. Yes, purple. Okay, maybe lilac. Reminds me of a bruise. The sky is bruised.

And then the sun elongates and becomes a red half-sun and drops. Gone. No green flash—sorry, Dad.

Time passes, no idea how long. It's getting dusky now. I glance up again and see Granne silhouetted in the doorway. She's gone then, inside, maybe to pour another glass, who knows. I'm all alone out here on the shore.

And that's when I hear something moving through the scrub behind me, toward me.

Granne has told me about the porcupines. Also the bear that shows up every few weeks. And the foxes. Coyotes. Raccoons. Bunnies.

I start to gather the quilt around me. Is it better to sit here without moving or make a run for it? I glance over my shoulder, hair starting to go up on the back of my neck (yes, this is a thing).

He comes over the scrubby point of land behind me and walks past me and out onto the sand. A boy with light hair over a gray (Gray? Blue? Hard to tell in the shadows) T-shirt and board shorts. Bare feet, I think.

And as he passes the corner of my quilt, just as he steps out onto the shore, he turns, raises his hand. All casual, as if he expected to find me sitting here.

"Hey," he says. That's it. He has a low, gruff sort of voice and that's all he says. Then he starts walking away down the beach.

I don't have time to respond. I don't have time to do anything, and then he's just a shape walking away from me. I watch him all the way down the beach and around the point by the house. A dark shape that just blends in with the dusk and shadows. And then—gone.

I wonder if Granne is watching. If she can even see this far in the twilight. Nope. She's not on the porch. I'm alone out here.

# What Granne doesn't know about me and books

"Time to get up. Come on, you. Up you get."

I could pretend to sleep through Granne's wake-up call at my door—actually, inside my room—but I force myself to crack my eyes open and look over at her, standing there dressed in jean capris and a loose gray T-shirt with a Blue Jays logo on it. My sporty grandmother, ready for action.

I make a sound like "urmmm" and nod to let her know I've heard her. Close my eyes.

"Come on, Larkin. Now." So easy to tell she was once a teacher. "I'll put the kettle on." And she's gone.

I roll onto my back and blink a few times. My jaw and nose hurt from where I had them pressed into the pillow. I must have been sleeping hard. I know I was dreaming hard—something scary, something … nope, gone. I open and close my jaw a few times to loosen it up. Nothing I can do for my nose.

She's in the kitchen, reading something on her iPad, but she looks up at me, nods. Approval? Or maybe just greeting. I really don't know. Haven't figured out the lingo yet when it comes to Granne. She points me to the teapot and toaster, set out together on the counter with bread, butter, and about five different jams.

"Help yourself. Toast and tea okay?"

"Yes, thanks."

At home I never eat breakfast. Just coffee. Lynette is always on me about that, about how unhealthy it is to start the day with just coffee. She's probably right, but of course that means I'm all about my one cup of coffee. Dad stays out of it. Or he did, anyway. It might be different now.

It was Lynette's idea that I should come to Nova Scotia and stay with Granne.

"You can't take her with you, Andrew."

"I know. I know." I'm in my room, but I think Lynette actually wants me to hear this conversation, without having to do it right in front of me. That's how she operates. Gets to Dad first, then backs him up when he talks to me, as if it was his idea in the first place. Letting him think he's doing the parenting.

"The last thing you need out there is the complication of presenting them with a beat-up granddaughter."

"I know, Lyn. I get it." And I squeeze myself tight inside because I hear the note of—what? Anger? Defeat?—in my dad's voice. *Messed-up daughter hanging out with parents of messed-up daughter. All in the family.*

My Vancouver grandparents are overwhelmed right now with my mother's latest admission to rehab. They won't want to see me like this. And Dad sounds like he can't cope, either.

"What about your mother?" Lynette says. "Couldn't she go stay there for a few weeks, while you go out west?"

Oh, God no, Dad. Don't send me away to Granne. I haven't been out there for six years. Her visits to Toronto are short and you're always there. I wouldn't know what to say or do around her. I'll be lost out on my own.

"Yeah. That's a thought."

And the thought becomes a thing and here I am, making toast and pouring too much sugar into my tea at Granne's house on the shore, while my father goes alone to Vancouver.

*What's bred in the bone.* I heard Lynette say that once, when I was lying in my room, thinking about what it would be like to be able to erase everything in my brain, like rebooting a computer.

And my father couldn't even find the words to reply.

"We'll be leaving in about half an hour. Does that give you enough time to get ready?" Granne clocks my pajama pants and hoodie. She means: *Does that give you enough time to make yourself presentable? So I can take you out in public and people won't stare? So I won't be embarrassed by you?*

"Sure ... no problem." I make toast, spread a thin layer of strawberry-rhubarb, and move to the table with my tea. No coffee this morning, apparently. (Again, I wonder how much my dad has told her.) The toast should taste wonderful but mostly makes me feel as if I'm going to gag. I get it down, though, looking out the window at the shore while she reads whatever on the iPad. Wonder if I might see "hey" boy go by again.

Nope. The shore is a crescent of red sand, with patches of seaweed, and waves inching up with the tide. Birds. No people.

Half an hour later, we're in town, parking in front of a red brick house at the corner of Water and Cumberland.

"Here it is," she says. "Your job for the summer."

My grandmother, retired high school principal, has become

an entrepreneur. And I'm her employee. That was the deal she made with my dad. Send Larkin, the screwed-up daughter/granddaughter to Tuttle Harbour for the summer, but by God, she'll have to earn her keep.

It's a store. No, a house. No, maybe a former store that was turned into a house and is now being turned back into a store. A wide covered porch—big enough for six or seven small tables with chairs (that's the plan, apparently) leads to a gingerbread-style screen door. And inside (I know this, because Granne went over the plans with me last night at the kitchen table, after I came in from the shore, still a bit buzzed about the "hey" boy, so not completely paying attention), an open room with space for more cozy tables and chairs, arm chairs, some tall tables, and stools at the windows. Beyond that, a long counter for coffee and tea urns, and a kitchen. A café. A small-town Starbucks wannabe. Granne's big retirement project.

But there's more.

Around the walls, shelves for books. Used books. For people to borrow, leaving a donation. For reading during your coffee break. And spaces to hang artwork. And a corner that can be turned into a performance nook for cool singer-songwriters or fiddlers or aspiring poets and writers to read on special literary open mic evenings. *An arts hub*, Granne calls it.

She gets surprisingly animated when she's describing it all to me, but I get stuck on the part where she tells me what my job is.

"You're going to be in charge of books," she says. "Acquiring, organizing, shelving, promoting."

Dad hasn't told her, apparently, about me and books. About the thing that started happening when I was maybe twelve. Mrs. Conway asking me to read out loud from *Silverwing*, and me, feeling my throat closing up, tears rising to the surface and spilling over. It's not that sad a book ... come on ... but words on the page, especially anything to do with families, or kids and parents (yes, even bat kids and bat parents), and I'm gone. My teachers try to be kind but they don't get it. Why is Larkin, the smart kid, the booky kid, getting choked up every time she reads? And I can't *not* read. It's school, after all, and we have to read books all the time. So after a while, it just becomes a thing: *Larkin, do you need a moment? Take a walk, dear, and come back when you're ready.* Grade 5, Grade 6, high school. *Shakespeare (oh, my God, Shakespeare! The Tempest! Romeo and Juliet!)*, the entire Grade 10 reading list. Yes, there I am, head down, as I scuttle to the Girls with a balled-up tissue in my hand, trying to stop gulping and weeping.

Me and books. Pretty sure my dad didn't mention this to her when they were setting up my job description for the summer, maybe because he was afraid she'd fire me before I got here—and then what?

But here I am, standing on the sidewalk outside the in-progress Tuttle Harbour Café and Reading Room, expected to start my first day on the job.

"Come on," says Granne, leading the way toward the sound of power tools.

There are no books inside. In fact, there's hardly anything inside, except a pale expanse of hardwood floor, lots of shiny new windows, a high, wood-beamed ceiling. And two guys wearing tool belts with their backs to us, on the other side of the long counter, fitting shelves to a wall in the open kitchen.

"Good morning, Billy," Granne calls out, as she lets the wooden screen door bang shut behind us, and the two guys glance up at us, pause in their power-tooling, and smile.

"Good morning, Mrs. D," says one guy, the older one. He's tall and skinny, wearing jeans and a work-stained gray T-shirt, graying hair, gray-stubbled, clearly not a shave-every-day kind of guy. Or get-a-haircut kind of guy, either. Faint whiff of cigarettes.

The other one is younger, and oddly like the first guy, except his dirty blond hair doesn't have any gray in it. Familiar.

No, it couldn't be.

"William Greenfield," says Granne. "Aren't you supposed to be working at the Co-op at this hour?"

William Greenfield grins without moving his hands from the shelf he's holding in place.

"Not until one o'clock. Afternoon shift today," he says. His voice is kind of gruff, raspy. Familiar.

Yup. It's "hey" boy.

And as it dawns on me, I see that he's grinning at me because he knows it's dawning on me.

"Meet my granddaughter, Larkin," Granne is saying. "Larkin, meet the rest of the work team. Billy Greenfield and son, William. Our colleagues. And, incidentally, our neighbors on the Point. They live just around the shore from us."

"Ah," I say. All is explained. "Hi."

"Welcome to Tuttle Harbour," says Billy, the dad. His voice is soft and kind of gruff, like his son's, and his glance flits away from me, as if he has trouble meeting my eyes. I think he's probably just shy. "Will said he thought he'd seen you out on the shore last night."

Will smiles at me, says "Hi." Friendly. Not shy, but not out there, either.

"Not sure 'colleagues' is the best word, though, Mrs. D," Billy says, turning back to Will and the shelf they're working on. "You're the boss, right?" He has that unmistakable Nova Scotia twang. It almost sounds put on.

"Well, I suppose," Granne agrees, but she says it lightly. A joke. "What's on our list for today, Billy?"

The shelf is screwed in place, and Billy steps away and starts talking to Granne about electrical boxes and stoves, while Will is doing something with the tools.

So I stand in the empty space and look around, turn slowly to take in the size of the room (surprisingly large—much larger than it looked from outside) and how bright it is with those windows, and what a great view of the street you'll get from the porch, and how there's room for lots of books on those shelves—and how am I going to handle this?

"Hey."

I jump. I didn't see him move out from the kitchen and he's now standing right beside me.

"Sorry," Will says. His eyes flick to my fading-but-still-green-and-purple periorbital hematoma, the yellow smudge on my jaw, and then flick away. "Didn't mean to scare you," he says.

I'm not sure if he means right now or last night, in the dark.

"It's okay," I say. Breathe in, out. Look away. Awkward pause.

"So you're in charge of books, eh?" he says after a moment. He's trying to be nice, welcoming, friendly, but all I can do is stand there and try to act normal. Not let him see that it's starting—that feeling of not being able to breathe, of being trapped somewhere small, like inside a car, with no way out, with something pressing down on me, hands holding me down.

And then I hear the door slam behind me and find myself out on the bright sidewalk, squinting, turning, running away from the Tuttle Harbour Café and Reading Room. Running away.

# Deck talk

"No, Larkin, I should be apologizing to you," Granne says.

We're on the deck again. After supper again. Wineglass again. Setting sun again.

She caught up to me in front of the Baptist Church, where I had to stop on the sidewalk and bend over, wheezing, shaking, trying to catch my breath. Granne can run when she wants to, and really well for the sixty-whatever-year-old she is. I catch a glimpse of her approaching, before squeezing my eyes shut, trying to suck oxygen in, trying to shut out the roaring in my ears, trying not to throw up.

Her arms go around me and I let it happen because I'm so afraid I'm going to black out, that I know at least she'll keep me from hitting the sidewalk. More bruises I don't need.

"Breathe, Larkin," she says to me, holding me, her voice firm and direct and unafraid. She's obviously seen teenagers have panic attacks before. "You're safe here. Just breathe and find yourself."

*Find yourself.*

Eventually, after forever, it passes, and she walks me back to the car, holding my arm the whole way, as if I'm ten again. I would be staggering without her there, so it's good. I'm aware of people walking past us, cars driving by. What do they think? Worse, what do they know? Right now, I don't care. All I care about is bringing air into my lungs so that the thundering of my heartbeats in my head will fade away—I know it will eventually—and I can open my eyes and be me again.

She helps me into the car and is gone for a moment. I open my eyes long enough to see her hurry back into the café, one hand on the door, holding it open as she says something to the Greenfields inside, and then she's back. Face calm and controlled, keys out.

"Let's go home," she says. "This can all wait until another day."

I can't speak yet, but when I can—later, after sleeping for hours, after a long, hot shower, after tea at the kitchen table, after a slow no-talking walk on the shore together, after supper, and now the two of us once again on the deck as the sun dips—I say: "I'm sorry about today, Granne."

I *am* sorry. Desperately, painfully, embarrassingly sorry. I don't even know how to explain it. Was it that boy, Will? Standing beside me? (Am I always going to be afraid of boys standing beside me now? That could be inconvenient.) Was it the whole books thing?

"No, Larkin. I should be apologizing to you," Granne says. Sips her wine. "Your father told me to tread lightly. I should have asked if you wanted to join me today. I'm sorry if I rushed you."

I pull up my knees and tuck my face into them, wrap my arms around my legs, as if I'm about to cannonball off the chair. "It's okay," I mumble, tightly bundled into myself.

"William was very upset that he'd done something to scare you," she says, all matter-of-fact. That's the principal in her, I guess. Keeping peace in the schoolyard.

I have no reply to that. He didn't do a thing to scare me— except maybe to be there. It horrifies me to think of Granne talking to the Greenfield father and son about me. But that's what happens when you mess up. Everyone talks about you.

*Did you hear about Larkin Day? Is it true about what happened …?*

We sit quietly, Granne sipping her wine and watching the

growing dusk, me cannonballed in place and unable to say any more. Then she shifts.

"I think I see William down on the shore," she says.

I peer down the shore, close to where I was camped last night on my quilt. Yes, I see him. He's sitting there on the sand, knees up, combing his fingers through the sand and shells and stones, flinging the odd one out toward the waves just starting to creep in over the sandbars. I'm sure I see him glance our way.

"I'm tired, Granne." I stand up and head for the door. "I think I'll go to bed and listen to some podcasts."

"Goodnight, Larkin," she says as the screen door snaps shut behind me. "Sleep well."

# News

"Grandma Sylvia and Grandpa John send their love," says Dad.

He sounds tired. I remember that my Vancouver grandparents are big on routines, like getting up every day at the same time and eating at the same time. Orderly. My Grandpa John is a university professor. Economics. Grandma Sylvia does volunteer work and goes out for lunch a lot.

"Give them my love." The expected and dutiful response from their only granddaughter who was too messed up to make the trip.

A silence as both of us are thinking about what to say next. Me: Any news? Him: No news or There's news.

"I hear you had a tough day yesterday," he says.

Right. I was pretty sure Granne would have reported in.

"Yeah. I'm okay. Don't worry about me."

"You know I worry."

"Don't worry, Dad. No big deal." Force myself to smile as I say it, so it comes out sounding lighter, more jokey. I'm pretty sure he's not fooled.

"Take care of yourself, Lark, eh?" He sounds exhausted.

"I will. You, too." A pause, then I can't help myself. "Any news?"

I want to know. I don't want to know.

"No change," he says. Tries to make it sound like good news.

We both know it's not.

# Sunset, Day 4

Okay. It's time.

He's been there every night. I see him from the porch, sometimes jogging by, down our shore and around the point behind us, then back again about a half-hour later. He stops at the end of our shore, just before heading over the hilly point of land that divides our shore from his, and wades out into the water, sometimes only knee deep. Sometimes less. He sits on the sand. Throws pebbles around. (Glances up at our house.) Goes back home.

I think he's stalking me but, really, I'm okay with it. I think it's time.

"Going for a walk on the shore," I say, all nonchalant. As if I haven't been thinking about this for two days now.

Granne nods. Takes another sip.

"Lovely night for it," she says. "Warm enough?"

I wave my hoodie at her—I brought it out with me after

supper and tucked it behind me on the chair as we settled in for our nightly after-dinner ritual.

"I'm good."

"Grab the quilt. Much cozier for sitting on the shore," she says.

So I do. The same routine as that first night. Find my spot near the end of the beach, spread out the quilt on the sand and sit, cannonball style, because it feels safe to be all curled into myself. Look out over the sandbars, which are high and smooth tonight, and think again about walking way out into the waves. Walking out and never turning around.

Glance up at Granne. Yup. Still there.

But it's different now, because the "hey" boy, William Greenfield, is also lurking somewhere in my thoughts. Maybe lurking in the darkness behind me right now. Right now, as I consider what it would be like to walk out over the sand and start drifting toward Prince Edward Island.

"Hey."

Like magic. He comes down off the hill of the point, through the beach grass, over a line of pebbles, and stops at the edge of the quilt.

So this is different, because last time he just kept going.

"Hi," I say, not looking at him. Take a deep breath, in and out.

"Great place to watch the sunset," he says.

"Yeah." Larkin of the silver tongue and quick mind. Larkin, the intelligent conversationalist.

He just stands there, doesn't try to sit, doesn't squat down, doesn't do anything. Just stands. I glance up quickly. He's watching the sunset.

"Never gets old," he says. "I'm out here practically every night, and I never get tired of it." I know that he knows that I know he's out here practically every night, and I think it's actually very nice of him not to mention that.

And then: "Hey, sorry about the other day at the café."

A response is required, so I take another deep breath and make myself speak.

"It's okay."

"Well, I know I said or did something to upset you, so I'm really sorry." I just shrug. "Never seen Mrs. D run so fast, though. Scared me a bit, actually."

That makes me laugh, since it's kind of what I thought, too.

He plops down on the sand beside my quilt, settles himself with his legs stretched out in front of him. Bare legs in board shorts. Tanned. Muscular and hairy in a young manly sort of way. Like the boys at school. The jock boys, in their gym shorts, stalking the hallways. Jonah and those guys …

*Look at the sky, Larkin. Look at the water. Is that a heron? Is that a star?*

We sit there for a few minutes, watching the sunset colors wash out across the sky, listening to the waves hissing out beyond the sandbars. I hope he can't tell that I'm doing the breathe-in and breathe-out exercise the mindfulness counselor taught me.

I glance up at the house. Granne is inside. I can see her in the window over the sink. Maybe rinsing out her wine glass.

I swallow. Take a breath. Go for it.

"It was mostly the books," I say. "It wasn't anything you did."

A pause. He's thinking about it and I'm glad I can't see his face.

"What books?"

"You know. The books I'm supposed to be looking after for the café."

"You're looking after the books? What—picking them out?"

I shrug. "That's what she told me. That I'd be in charge of getting and organizing the books. I'd be in charge of books. It's supposed to be my summer job."

He starts running his hand through the sand at the edge of the quilt, raking his fingers through the pebbles and shells. Back and forth, rhythmic and mindless.

"And you're not happy about that?" he asks. "You don't like books?"

How to explain to someone who doesn't know you—doesn't know you at all—that you're so messed up, you can't even look after books?

So I decide to do something I haven't done for a long time. I leap. Why not? He's already seen me in freak-out mode, so I leap right in. Just like plunging out into those waves and making for Prince Edward Island.

"Books make me cry."

"Books make you cry?"

"Yes. When I read books, some books, I cry."

He doesn't believe me. I know this because he laughs, as if I'm going to laugh with him and say, *I know, eh? Books suck!*

But I don't. This is a test for William Greenfield. If he gets this, I will be okay sitting here on the shore with him and he won't scare me, even with his muscular, hairy legs and boy hands and obvious familiarity with power tools. And if he makes fun of me, or doesn't understand—then, well, I'll be packing up my quilt and going home.

"So, you mean, like those sappy romance novels?" he asks.

I nod.

"How about *Hunger Games*? Or that *Twilight* crap?"

Shrug, nod. God, yes. All those dead people. All that horrible and often creepy stuff that people to do each other.

"*To Kill a Mockingbird? Stone Angel? Handmaid's Tale?*" The classic high school reading list. Nod. Nod. Nod.

He thinks for a minute, then: "*Harry Potter?*"

I nod slowly and meaningfully. "Buckets."

He nods, too. "Yeah. That whole Snape storyline, eh?"

It's dark now. The sun is well and truly down but there's still light in the sky. Enough light to see my way back down the beach toward Granne's house where the lights are on in the kitchen and living room. She's probably watching the news by now. That's her evening ritual.

Or she might be there at the window in the dark mudroom, staring down the shore, watching for me. Wondering if it was such a good idea to let me out with the cozy quilt at sunset.

"I should go," I say.

We both stand up. I give the quilt a shake, then bundle it up in a lump.

"You okay along the shore?"

"Yes, thanks." I'm tired now. Running out of words. I don't want him to come with me.

"K. Maybe see you tomorrow," he says.

"Sure. Maybe. Bye."

I turn away, hugging the quilt like a baby, and try to walk normally down the shore, but it's difficult in the dark, on the sand, so I actually stumble a bit. I don't look back and he doesn't say anything. Maybe he's standing there watching me, I don't know. Maybe he's already climbing back over the point to his own house.

Then—

"Hey!" he calls out. "There's a campfire on the back shore tomorrow night. Some kids from school. We could go if you want."

I stop and turn, pick him out as a dark shape near the top of the point. His fair hair shows up in the light coming from the twilight sky. I don't say anything, but I stop there, wave one arm over my head twice. Hope he knows that means, "Okay."

Hope he knows that means that I have decided I trust him.

# Becca

"We've had some donations," says Granne.

We're standing in a storage room at the back of the café. Actually, she's standing inside the little room, and I'm standing in the doorway, one foot in and one foot out, in case I get the urge to run again.

So far so good.

Donations. No kidding. There must be over twenty mid-sized packing boxes here. And shopping bags of varying sizes, toppling over with paperbacks, hardcovers, picture books. Yes, I see *Magic Tree House*, and the Harry Potter series (oh, God, no, don't get me started).

"Once I heard the library was going to be closed, I lobbied for some of the collection, but the County said those books would be redistributed, so people just stepped up and started bringing me donations. Very kind," she adds, although her voice sounds like she wants to smack someone. The County, whoever that is, probably.

"Wow. That's a lot of books."

She glances at me. "Yes, it is. And you'll be sorting them all and setting them out on the shelves."

I can do this. Like that little train from the book my mother used to read to me at bedtime—*I think I can, I think I can*. My mother, and books …

"Right?" she asks, using her teacher voice to haul me back. As if she's making sure I'm going to get my homework done and handed in tomorrow.

"Right." Maybe this is the moment to tell her? I'm just getting myself ready, taking a breath, when we're interrupted.

"Anne? Are you here?"

It's a woman's voice, calling from the front door. I see Granne smile and move into welcome mode, slip past me, and head back into the main room. Gives me a head nod, which means *Follow me.*

"Becca, hi."

I don't want to follow, of course. I want to test myself here in this little storage room. I want to stand here, breathing in and out, looking at all the bags and boxes and spines and covers of books peeking out at me, and just see what happens. See if images of me and my mother and trips to the library start to take over. See if I can take it.

My ears start to ring a little, and there's the thump-thump-*thump* of my heart starting its reverb in my head.

I decide maybe meeting Granne's friend might be a better idea. I back out of the storage room and move into the space behind the counter, where I reach out with both hands and just grab hold of the edge of the countertop. *Count to twenty.* That's what the mindfulness counselor told me to do. *Count. Breathe. Feel my feet solid on the ground. Feel my hands gripping the counter top.*

"And this is Larkin," says a woman's voice. A soft, low voice, friendly. Warm. Safe, even.

I open my eyes.

She's standing with Granne in the empty café, watching me as if she knows exactly what's going on in my head. As if she knows exactly why my hands are gripping the countertop, and doesn't think it's strange. She's wearing skinny jeans and a flowy tunic thing that might actually be tie-dyed, but I don't know for sure because it's her face that I'm drawn to. Her eyes. Her eyes are a piercing light blue, maybe even gray, highlighted with dark lashes. The effect is startling—two bright lights in a smooth, pale face, surrounded by a cloud of black hair. A few silver streaks.

"Larkin, hi. I'm so pleased to see you again," she says.

"Hi." I say it before even registering her words, then ...

Wait. What? *Again?*

"Larkin, this is Becca Patriquin," says Granne, clearly taking pity on me. "She met you when you were about six months old."

When I was six months old, my parents brought me to visit Granne. I know this because there are photos in our family album (the album that we stopped adding to around the time my mother left for Vancouver). The Show and Tell trip, Dad called it. Whenever this visit came up in conversation, my mother would raise her eyebrows and take another sip of whatever was in her hand at the moment (tea, coffee, beer, wine, other). Photos show baby me squinting out from a stroller on the road in front of Granne's house, and lying on a blanket on the shore under a beach umbrella. Sitting on Granne's lap waving some elephant toy around. My dad looking all buff and fit as he dangles my feet in the waves, my mouth in a perfect "O" and my eyebrows sky-high as I look down at the water. Maybe I'm already wondering what's under there that I should be afraid of? There's a photo of my mother in a bathing suit, lounging on a beach chair with a paperback, wearing a stylish sunhat, and looking like a model. No photos of this Becca person, though.

"You wouldn't remember me," this Becca person says now. "You were a baby, and your dad and mom came back home to show you off."

*Came back home.* What?

"Becca and your dad went all through school together," Granne says.

"Oh." I nod as if this explains everything. But it doesn't, and Becca seems to understand that I'm not quite taking this all in, that I'm still gripping the countertop. She smiles and turns away to look at the room.

"This looks fantastic, Anne."

Becca revolves slowly, taking in the windows, the shiny hardwood floor, the shelves. They're not looking at me anymore, so I breathe in and out again, slowly, release my grip on the countertop, and lean my arms on it. Just like a normal person.

"Billy's done a wonderful job." Becca waves an arm at the windows. "So much better than those casement things that were in here before. And the shelves are beautiful, too."

"Ready for books, when Larkin gets them sorted." Granne nods, doesn't look at me. She knows I'm there, listening.

Becca throws a smile over her shoulder at me, though, and then she steps toward a space on the wall between shelves. An empty space. She stands there and looks at it for a moment, then turns to Granne and says: "So, here? Is that what you're thinking? And there, and there?" Now she's revolving again, which makes her tunic-y thing flow around her. The effect is mesmerizing— like a dancer pirouetting in some floaty costume on a stage. But Becca Patriquin doesn't look as if she's showing off. This just seems to be the way she moves. "And the big one on that dividing wall, there?"

The big what? No idea what she's talking about, so I just watch them, relieved to be here in the background, leaning on the counter, breathing normally, and not feeling the urge to run.

"Exactly," Granne nods, also looking at the empty spaces on the wall.

"Okay, leave it with me." Becca is still staring at the space for the big one, whatever the big one is. All I see is bare white wall.

"Grand opening is a week today, so that gives you some time to go through your collection," says Granne.

Thursday. A week. Seven days to get those piles of books onto the shelves.

"No problem. I have lots of stuff on hand, and a few in progress, too." Becca moves toward the door and then turns to look back at me. Me, looking all cool and relaxed behind the counter, as I try to imagine myself getting these books organized by a next Thursday. "See you, Larkin. Come for a visit anytime. I can tell you a few stories about what a troublemaker your dad was in high school."

I do manage to smile, maybe even nod, maybe even laugh a little, but I actually have no idea why she thinks I would want to do that. I can barely get through a conversation with Granne and Hey Boy. And if she knew Dad in high school, it could be all weird—like, what if they went to the prom together or something?

Becca and her tie-dye tunic float toward the door, where she pauses and looks back at me.

"It's really lovely to see you again, Larkin," she says.

And then she's gone.

Granne must see the look on my face because she laughs a little.

"Becca lives up the road from us. She's a fabric artist," she says. "She does exquisite rug hooking, so she's going to provide some art for the walls."

Ah. The fascination with bare spaces between shelves is now explained.

"And she went to school with my dad?"

"Yes, indeed. Becca and your dad, and Billy Greenfield too. All in the same class at school." She shakes her head, as if remembering something scary. "All in my English class."

I've always known my dad had Granne as a teacher at Tuttle Harbour District High School, which sounds like a perfect description of torture to me (having your own parent as a *teacher*?), but now, after meeting Becca—and tool-belt-guy Billy, another classmate—images of my dad as a teenager are starting to creep into my mind, and I don't really like it.

"Come on, let's get at it," says Granne, striding toward me. Me and the storage room full of books. I'm almost happy to follow her.

# Campfire

Dad calls just after supper.

"I saw Mom today."

Silence, as I think about what I should say or ask. Or if I even want to say or ask anything. He doesn't wait for me to figure it out.

"She's pretty fragile, Lark. Not talking a lot." He pauses. Maybe waiting for me to say something. I don't. "But she did ask about you. I told her you had a job in Tuttle Harbour for the summer."

Would she even remember Tuttle Harbour? She hasn't been here since that Show and Tell trip and, since then, she's killed off a few brain cells. I'm actually surprised she remembered to ask about me.

Time to change the subject.

"How are you?" I ask him. He sounds like someone who's really tired and trying to make his voice sound like he's not.

"Good, honey. Good. Eating too much of Grandma Sylvia's shortbread cookies, if you know what I mean."

I do. My Vancouver grandmother is big on the baking. With Dad there, she'll have plates full of sweet treats sitting out to keep him stuffed and quiet. Eating shortbread is more socially acceptable than talking about drug-damaged family members. Grandma Sylvia has life all figured out, and the answer is shortbread.

If I were there, Dad and I would go together to visit Mom at the treatment center where she's staying now. And then we'd come home, eat shortbread and Nanaimo bars and banana bread, and have each other's back while Grandma Sylvia tried to make touristy plans for us to visit the museum, the art gallery, the aquarium. Walks around Stanley Park. Lunch out. Touring the neighborhood with Grandpa John and Ernie, his yappy Jack Russell terrier, so that the neighbors will see that we're just a normal family.

Except for the drug-addicted daughter-wife-mother part.

"How long will you stay?" I ask. I know his plan is to stay for at least the whole month of July. We were going to stay for the whole summer, to be there when or if she's released back into the care of my grandparents, whenever that is.

"Not sure, Lark. Not sure. Couple of weeks at least, I think," he says. "She's kind of tired and weak, you know? That was a bad episode back there in April."

Phone call in the middle of the night from Vancouver. They'd found her after two months missing. Alive, not just another dead drugged-up stick-woman on the street. Saved, Grandpa John said. Back into the expensive rehab facility they've been paying for on and off for years. Maybe this time it'll work.

Yeah, April was a bad month for our family. And then June ...

"So what are you up to? Granne keeping you busy?"

"Yeah, getting things organized at the café," I say, happy to move on to a new topic, even if this one is also a bit dangerous. "Organizing the books."

"Books. Good for you." He pulls out his cheerleader voice. "How's it looking?"

"Pretty good, actually. It's all shiny and new, you know? New floors and windows and all these bookshelves. New kitchen area."

"I remember that building," he says. "An old guy named Waterson lived there, and then it was an accountant's office for a while. Granne said Billy Greenfield's doing the work, and Billy's a wiz at that stuff. She must be the talk of the town, reviving that old place."

"I don't know." Is Granne the talk of the town? Or maybe it's her sidewalk-sprinting granddaughter. "But, hey, I met a friend of yours today."

"A friend of mine?"

"Becca somebody."

He laughs. "Becca Patriquin? Oh, man. I haven't seen her for years. We were at school together. Becca and Billy and me. The kids from the Point. I thought she got married and moved away. How did you meet her?"

So I tell him about Becca and the empty spaces on the walls, how she's an artist now. He knew she'd gone into teaching, into the arts, he says. She was always drawing or making stuff. He always tried to be in her group when they had to do group work, because you knew the presentation would be fantastic ...

A knock on the sliding door and I can hear Granne talking to someone in the kitchen.

"Come in, come in. She's just talking to her father."

"Hey, Dad? Can we talk tomorrow? I gotta go now. I'm going to a campfire with some kids here." It sounds so normal and safe.

(It is normal and safe, right?) But my father puts on his hearty voice when he tells me to go have fun, great that I'm meeting some local kids. Great, Larkin. Great.

And then: "Be careful, eh, Lark? Take care."

"I will. Don't worry."

Don't worry. Ha. It's all he does. And, let's face it, why not?

"Love you, Dad."

"Love you too, Lark."

We click off and I need a minute before turning away from the living room window and heading into the kitchen, where Granne and Will are talking about the fire and who will be there. I picture my dad all the way across the country, taking a minute to worry about me and everything else.

"Hey, ready to go?" asks Will as I appear at the door. He's in jeans and a T-shirt, carrying a hoodie, looking very tall and big all of a sudden, and I have to force myself to reply.

"Yeah, sure. Let me just grab another layer."

In my room, I close my eyes and put my hands over my hot face. *Breathe, Larkin.* Yes, my heart is beating loudly in my ears. *You can do this, Larkin.* Geez. I hate myself for a minute. Hate Jonah and that car. *Don't go there.*

"You don't have to go if you'd rather stay home," says Granne quietly from the doorway, so I drop my hands from my face, grab my mom's old Queen's sweatshirt, and turn.

"No, it sounds like fun. I'm good." I move past her toward the kitchen and Will. Toward this evening spent with other kids. Toward this normal thing.

I can have just one normal thing, can't I? Can't I?

"Ready?" says Will.

"Yup. Let's go. See you later, Granne."

"William Greenfield—" Granne starts, but he cuts her off. Holds up his hand.

"Don't worry, Mrs. D. We won't be that late." He waves his sweatshirt back and forth. "Got my flashlight in here."

"And who's going to be there, may I ask?"

"Casey, of course. Beth. Vin. Mick. Probably Chelsea. That's probably it."

"The usual suspects, then." Granne nods, still standing there at the kitchen sink, watching us. Watching me.

"Fine. Well, off you go. Take care," she says to me, echoing my father.

"Yup, I will."

And as I turn to follow Will out the door, I know she's seeing the green-yellow bruise around my eye. I know what she's thinking.

Because I'm thinking it too.

*Is this a good idea?*

# New girl in town

Our walk along the shore is less a walk and more of a climb over an obstacle course.

The tide is way out, but instead of heading out toward the sandbars, Will leads me on the shortest route, closer to the bank. There are lots of red boulders jumbled around, with tidal pools full of seaweed and shells and hermit crabs skittering around. And slippery flat rocks everywhere. Tricky. And just to make it even more fun, the sun sets just as we come down off the path from Granne's house, which means it's getting dusky and dark.

But it's a wide, wild open space, with the huge sky in shades of blue, pink, and purple, and the water past the sandbars stretching all the way to Prince Edward Island. When I stop for a minute and look out at the strait, I can see red lights blinking off and on from a communications tower somewhere over there. The night might be closing in but the sounds are soft and whispery around me. I'm okay. So far, okay. If I could just get over these rocks without wiping out.

Will hops, steps, and saunters along as if he's on a sidewalk, but I'm unsure of my footing, careful where I step.

"You'll get used to it," he says, walking back to join me at one point as I stand on a rock, calculating the risk of choosing either the route to the right or left: one high and dry, requiring leaps from rock to rock, the other requiring me to get my feet wet. I go high.

"It's going to be an interesting trip back in the dark," I say. I'm thinking of his little flashlight and the two of us picking a route across the rocks. Actually, I'm trying not to think about that.

"Ha, no. We'll come the back way," he says, waving one arm up over the rocks and sagging pines that hang onto the high eroding bank beside us. "Through the cow pasture back to the road. There's a lane there. Maybe Casey can drive us."

"Drive us?"

Also, who's Casey? And Beth, and Vin and Mick and Chelsea? *The usual suspects*, Granne called them.

I'm back on the low flat rocks now and we're able to walk, sort of, side by side. I keep my eyes focused on my next step. The worst of the big boulders is behind us now and the shore is mostly flat-but-slippery stepping stones, surrounded by sand and seaweed.

"Yeah, Casey has a souped-up ATV kind of thing. They use them on the farm to check on the cows and stuff, but Casey likes to book it up and down the road from time to time," Will says. "The fire pit is here on the shore, at the end of the lane between the fields. They made this kind of a picnic park, you know, for lobster boils, and hanging out and swimming. Family picnics. Big family, the Henwoods."

"So, this fire we're going to, it's with this Casey guy? Casey Henwood?" I want to know what I'm getting into. Actually, I'm starting to regret getting into anything, but I've decided to trust Will Greenfield, and I feel almost ... maybe ... sort of ... okay ... walking out here in the growing darkness with him. Maybe because he gets my book problem and felt bad about me running away from him that day at the café. Also, I know Granne will kill him if anything happens to me.

"Yeah. Casey and some people from school." He points up ahead. "See them? There."

I've been so focused on my feet and not wiping out on the slippery rocks and embarrassing myself that I've hardly looked up. But now I do. We've come around a point of land and there it is, up on a grassy area above the shore: a fire, and people standing around it. Somebody waves and calls out to us.

"Greeny! What took you?"

Will leads the way over the rocks and looks back to make sure I'm following. Or not wiping out. One or the other.

"Hey, guys."

I follow him up a rough set of wooden stairs built into the bank, and then there's that awkward moment when all these people who know each other stop talking and look at the new girl.

"This is Larkin," says Will. "She's here, staying with her grandmother. You know, Mrs. D."

"Oh, yeah. Hi, Larkin." One of the guys is standing there with his arm draped over the shoulders of a short girl with dyed blonde hair. Couple, obviously. "I heard you were coming this summer."

"Casey," Will says, turning to me. "This is his farm we're burning up."

Casey, our host. Part of the Henwood farm dynasty.

"Yeah, we missed you and your pyro skills, Greeny."

The girl with him laughs when he says *Greeny*, because he says it in a way that makes me think it's not a friendly nickname.

Schoolyard stuff. Will ignores him and starts introducing me to everyone else. Beth, the blonde, who smiles big-time at Will but not so much at me (there's a story there, for sure). A tall red-haired girl named Chelsea, standing with two more guys, Vin and Mick, who look like twins in their shorts, T-shirts, and Jays ball caps.

I nod, say hi, hey, wave, make suitable new girl motions. And stick close to Will. Thank goodness it's getting darker now and no one can see my yellow-green eye decorations.

"Cooler's in the back of the bike," says Casey, and I see that he's holding a beer can and gesturing toward the ATV parked in the shadows behind us.

"No, thanks. Gotta work tomorrow morning early," says Will.

"Right," Casey laughs. "Friday morning is truck day at the Co-op. Gotta get those shelves stocked."

"Yup. Hey, Mick, did you win last night?" and Will turns away to talk to one of the T-shirt guys about, I think, baseball, and I'm momentarily standing alone and starting to hear the sound of my own heart in my ears, because now I see that everyone else is holding something—a can of beer, a Mike's Hard, a plastic cup of something that might be plain Coke but probably isn't—and

Beth has left Casey's side and is walking toward me and saying, "Hey, Larkin, want something?" and because I'm now standing alone here, feeling the dark closing in around me, I say, "Sure, thanks." Stand there while Beth says something to Casey and he goes back to the ATV and fills a plastic cup. He brings it back, but it's Beth who takes it and hands it to me. A plastic cup with some mystery drink in it, and I know right then I really should have stayed home with Granne and watched the stars come out.

But I take a big swallow, and it tastes so good and goes down easily. Take another. Smile at Casey. Ignore Beth's stink eye. Look over at Will, who has stopped talking to the boys and is watching me, too. Maybe he's worried Granne will disapprove, but I just raise my cup and drink to show him it's all good. I'll be okay. I'll be okay now.

# Morning after

Granne bangs on the door. Twice. Hard.

"Time to get up, Larkin. We're leaving in half an hour."

Don't move. If I move, I might throw up.

Later she opens the door and asks, "Well? Are you coming?" and I just lie curled up away from her, quilt pulled tight around me, willing her to go away, which she does.

Sleep.

Later still, I wake up to the sound of the front door closing—not slamming, exactly, but definitely closing with a firm, angry grandmotherly smack—and her car starting up. Hear the crunching of tires on stone, receding as she moves down the driveway. Hear the tide coming in or going out over the sandbars—I've totally lost track of time and space. There's a noisy family of crows in the pines outside my window. Gulls, far off.

I lie still, eyes closed. Yeah, I'll just stay like this for a while.

# Afternoon after

I get up around noon. Mostly because I really have to pee, but also because I've been awake for ten minutes and realize that I'm not going to be sick.

At some point during the morning, I rolled over and saw a tall glass of water on my nightstand and have been downing that during my brief sessions of being awake and feeling like moving. Maybe that helped.

So I get up, which feels horrible but could be worse. I know this from experience. And I find clean clothes and go have a shower. Hurray for steamy mirrors, I say. No need to make eye contact with the girl looking back at me.

And then tea and toast. The house is quiet, peaceful, even, and as long as I don't think about Granne driving off this morning without me, I'm actually feeling okay, like I can cope with whatever comes next. Because whatever comes next is bound to be bad.

But for now, I'm just sitting at the kitchen table, carefully chewing and swallowing cinnamon toast and drinking tea. The tide is high, so lots of wave action over the red sand and rocks and seaweed, but it's soothing to watch. Soothing to listen to through the open sliding door off the kitchen.

And then I hear another sound. A car on the road, coming this way. Granne.

I guess it was too good to last.

I just keep eating and watching the waves, waiting for her to crack the front door open and march in, and do whatever it is she's going to do to me after I came in last night, bouncing off the doorway to the kitchen, where she was waiting for me. Bouncing off a few more walls on the way to the bathroom, where I threw up and splashed some water on my face. And then on to my room, where I peeled off my clothes and fell into bed and went to sleep. Or passed out … but I prefer to think of it as going to sleep.

I remember everything. I wasn't that far gone in Beth's non-stop supply of whatever was in those cups. I remember that I didn't look at Granne's face, just her feet (she was barefoot, sitting there at the kitchen table, watching me). I remember that I said "Hi, Granne. 'Night, Granne" as I teetered by her toward the bathroom.

I remember that she didn't make a single sound. She just sat there and watched Larkin do what Larkin does best.

But there's always a morning after. I know this from experience. My mother—well, too many images there to drag up. And this afternoon is the morning after, and Granne is on her way (sound of car door slamming shut) to deliver my morning after, here, this afternoon, in her kitchen on the shore.

Only it's not Granne who comes up the steps of the back deck and appears at the sliding kitchen door.

It's Will.

Will, wearing the red T-shirt and dark jeans that all the Co-op workers wear, standing on the other side of the screen door and making no move to come in.

"Hey," he says.

"Hi."

Talking through a screen door is weird. Also, I can't make myself look at his face so I just stare at the Co-op logo on his shirt.

"How're you feeling?"

"Okay. Fine." Also stupid, and not fine, but he probably knows that.

"Mrs. D told me to come get you," he says, still making no

move to come in. He's holding his car keys in one hand and swinging them against his other. "I just have to go change, then I'll come back and get you, okay?"

I nod. "Okay. I'll be ready."

"Ten minutes," he says, nods, and turns away.

I hear him run down the steps. The car door, engine starting, and he books it out of the yard and down the driveway.

Okay. Business as usual, apparently.

I take my dishes to the sink and go to the bathroom to brush my teeth and try to recognize that girl in the mirror. I make my bed and stuff my phone in my little courier bag with my wallet, brush.

Granne doesn't lock her door, so no keys to worry about. I go out through the kitchen and sit on the top step of the deck, where I can watch the shore but also see any cars coming up the road to our driveway. Ready for Will and thinking:

I'm glad it's Will who's driving me into town to face Granne and all those books today. But something tells me, Will isn't so thrilled about it.

# Drive

He doesn't say anything as I get in. Doesn't say anything as he turns the car around and heads down the road, past the entrance to his long driveway next door and the scrubby bush and pines that hide his house from view. Doesn't say anything until we're passing the Henwood farm, just before the turn onto the road to town.

I'm frozen, thinking about saying something to break the silence, not sure if he's angry at me for acting like a jerk and dragging him along on my bad ride last night. (Yes, he's the one who helped me out of Casey's ATV and practically carried me up the driveway, who propelled me up the steps of the deck and opened the sliding door there, where Granne was waiting in the kitchen. Words were said, although I can't remember what they were, and then he was gone.)

In his shoes, I would be very pissed.

But it's hard to tell. He's not talking. He's just driving, all calm and quiet as if nothing is different. But of course, everything is different, because now he knows this thing about me. He's seen me in action. Twice. The messed-up girl. The girl who can't handle close spaces and random books and new people. The girl who drinks too much.

And then, just as we pass the Henwood place, with its multiple silos and enormous barn and big *House & Homes* cover-photo perfection, he says, without looking at me:

"Yeah, so maybe you should be careful around Beth and Casey."

I turn my head away from him and watch the field on my right, stretching down to the water, and don't see a thing because my eyes are full of tears. Of all the things he might say to me, this isn't what I expected.

"Yeah. Maybe." It's all I can manage. My throat feels like it's closing.

He turns up the radio for some golden oldie my dad would know the name of, and he taps out a rhythm on the steering wheel.

"Classic song, eh?" I can hear him smiling, driving along.

"Yeah," I say, managing to smile a little, too. "Classic."

# Work day

So, it's not terrible.

First, Granne just looks up and says, "Larkin. You're here. Good." And that's it. She's going through paperwork. Forms, maybe orders, I don't know, and she says this and then immediately looks back down at her papers, waves an arm toward the little storage room full of books in bags.

"You could start sorting those by genre," she says without looking back at me. Busy and kind of brushing me off.

But this is okay with me. I mean, it could have been so much worse. She could have stood there glaring at me, all disappointed-teacher-like, and delivered a lecture about last night, about being late for work. And all in front of Billy, who's down on the floor, nailing in trim or something. And, of course, Will is already strapping on his tool belt and getting to work on drawer handles in the kitchen. Or maybe he's just getting out of the line of fire.

But there's no fire. Maybe Granne's saving it for later, I don't know, but for now, all I have to do is get one of the bags or boxes from the storage room, go through the books, and sort them by genre.

I should be able to do this. I should be able to. I can do this. (My insides still feel a bit funny. Head still fuzzy. But I'm here, and Will just looked over at me and gave me a look that says something like, *Yikes. Tough assignment from the teacher.* I can do this.)

The first bag is full of kids' books, mostly picture books and some of those hard-board books. A few look familiar but I don't read them (well, okay, maybe a little. *In the great green room* ...). I just breathe, look, sort. Make piles. Breathe, look, sort.

Suddenly there's a Sci-Fi novel in there, too, with a guy on the cover, looking like a tough cowboy carrying a super-loaded futuristic rifle, and followed by a female with a head like a fox. Too weird. I picture some sleep-deprived parent, no brain cells left to process real literature, picking this up to read while waiting for Baby to stop crying and go to sleep. It goes into a new pile.

And a bunch of new piles join Cowboys in Space: romance, mystery, fantasy, historical fiction, biography. The afternoon slips by. Billy takes a smoke break. Will runs to the bakery and brings us back cinnamon rolls. (I can't eat mine. Way too sweet. But he brings me and Granne tea, too, and it tastes so good.) Granne makes a few phone calls, setting up the delivery of kitchen equipment next week. Hammering. Sanding. Everyone busy and the hours go by. Here I am, surrounded by piles of books, and I'm still breathing. Still here.

"I'll help you package them up and label the boxes," says Granne, and I look up to see that Will and his dad are packing up. Granne's papers are out of sight. It's closing time, and I didn't even notice any kind of time at all.

"Nice work, Larkin," she says, and nods at me.

Gold star for Larkin. I have just survived my first day on the job, without hyperventilating, throwing up, running out the door and down the street, or generally messing up and embarrassing myself.

"See you tomorrow, Mrs. D," says Billy, heading to the door. He shuffles a little when he walks. Always smells faintly of cigarettes. But he turns as he holds the screen door open for Will, and gives me a crooked half-smile. "See you tomorrow, Larkin."

Will waves, too, and they're out the door. I hear their tool belts thump into the truck bed, and doors open and thunk closed. The engine rumbles and they're gone.

"Well," Granne stands there for moment, watching them through the screen door, then turning to look at me. "Let's get these piles packed into boxes. Then home. You must be tired."

Tired? I guess that's a word for it, sure.

"Yeah, I am."

She gives me a look that says she knows exactly just how tired I am, and why, and picks up one of the now-empty boxes. Starts filling it with my biography pile. We don't talk at all as we work but it's okay.

# Evening visitor

I thought I'd be wiped but I'm not. I'm a little buzzed, actually, after this good day at work among the piles of books.

It's after supper now and Granne has decided to work at the kitchen table, instead of sitting outside with the usual glass of wine and evening show from the shore.

She has her computer open, and file folders full of I don't know what—things she's ordered for the café, official registration forms, legal stuff—beside her. I think she's in business mogul mode and not very sociable, so I go sit alone on the back deck, out of sight of the road.

But I'm antsy tonight. I figured there'd be some kind of follow-up to my spectacular fail last night. Maybe it's not going to happen. It's like I get one free pass, and I'm off the hook because, once I finally got there, I survived an afternoon at the café without embarrassing myself. Or her.

Fine. I could just go walk on the shore by myself. Maybe Will is out, too, and he'll come over and we can, I don't know, walk up and down the shore and talk about stuff that doesn't have to do with books, drinking, messing up ...

The front doorbell rings and I hear Granne push back her chair.

"Were you expecting anyone?" she calls out to me.

"Nope."

For a second, I think it might be Will, but of course, he would come to the back door, the deck where I am. He's on familiar ground here.

I lean on the railing and look out at the tide, just reaching the sandbars. Over there is Prince Edward Island, still calling to me.

"Casey Henwood," I hear Granne say in her teacher voice. No, in her *school principal* voice.

Casey? Here?

Last night at the bonfire-and-beer extravaganza I talked to Casey quite a bit. Beth was there most of the time, too, draping herself on his non-beer-holding arm and pressing herself close to his side. *He's mine, so back off, New Girl.* That was the message, loud and clear. Fine with me. I wasn't interested in hooking up with Casey, but he certainly seemed interested in me. Lots of questions about home in Ontario. About Mrs. D's café. Friendly but harsh guy-bashing of Will. *Greeny*, he called him. As Beth kept filling my plastic cup, as the sun set and the wind dropped and the fire crackled, and it all kind of fuzzed over. I liked it. I liked it maybe too much, though. Then, much later, a wild ride with Casey up the bumpy lane through the cow fields, bouncing off the sides and hanging onto the little door, and being helped out of the ATV by Will. (Where did he come from? Did he ride in that little storage space in the back?) Propped up and staggering, giggling, up the road to our driveway. The deck stairs, Will opening the door, and Granne waiting.

I remember that part.

And here's Casey. Great. There's a muted conversation going on in the living room near the front door.

Maybe I can slip off the deck and book it down to the shore before I'm expected to participate. Because surely he's here to see me, not Granne.

Actually, though, the conversation seems to be going on longer than you would expect for someone coming to see me.

"Larkin, could you come in here, please?"

Summoned to the principal's office. Shit.

Casey is standing just inside the door with a tight little smile, and his head tilted forward a little, as if he's afraid he's going to get a smack from somewhere. Maybe from Mrs. D.

Granne watches me as I come in through the kitchen and take up a position in the living room, not too close, not too far, just right for an exit, if required.

"Casey has something to say to you."

Oh God. I know that teacher intro. This is an apology.

"Hey, Larkin, I'm really sorry about last night. I know we all kind of overdid it and it wasn't fair to you at all, and I'm so, so sorry that we weren't more careful. It wasn't a great way to welcome someone new to the Point, and we all know we're supposed to be better than that and that our parents trust us to be better, so, yeah, I'm really sorry."

This guy is good. But okay, what I am I supposed to say? I look down at the floor because it's just too embarrassing to look at him, with Granne standing there, supervising the schoolyard post-incident scene.

"Larkin?" Granne, on yard duty.

"Thanks. It's okay," I manage to say and glance up at him.

And he's grinning behind Granne's back. Yeah, he's grinning because he's that smart guy who knows how to say exactly what the teacher wants him to say. He's sending me a message: *Yeah, whatever, eh?*

"Fine," says Granne, and I know from her voice she's not fooled by groveling Casey, either. "Now, I have to get back to work. Will you stay for a minute, Casey, or do you have to get back?"

"Oh, I was wondering if maybe you'd like to go for a walk on the shore," he says, looking at me. "If that's okay." And now he's turning those big brown eyes on Granne.

"Fine with me. Larkin? A little fresh air wouldn't hurt you."

They're both standing there, waiting for me to say something.

*Yeah, so maybe you should be careful around Beth and Casey.*

Will's voice in my head. But hey, I just survived an afternoon surrounded by books. I have total confidence in my ability to handle this guy with his sneaky grins and his attitude and his cranky girlfriend.

"Sure. Good," I say. "Let me just get my hoodie."

# Mysteries on the Shore

"Put your foot here, see?" Casey digs his bare foot into the mushy circle of sand. "Where the bubbles are."

He pulls his foot out and nods at me. My turn.

I hesitate, of course, because there may be slimy, prickly, biting creatures or something worse in there and he could just be messing with me.

But his foot emerges unscathed, no teeth marks. Okay, I'm probably being a wuss.

I reach with my toes to test it first, and immediately I feel something.

"It's so cold."

"I know, eh? The spring is way down there under the sand, and it just bubbles up through all these layers."

I step in closer and burrow down into the red sand with my foot, the way he did. I feel the difference as the fresh-water spring turns this small circle in the hard, grainy red sandbar into a pocket of mush.

Really cold mush. I pull my foot out and watch as the sand settles again in the little pool and the bubbles break through.

"Very cool," I say.

"I thought you'd like that." He takes another turn stirring the pool of cold bubbly sand around with his foot, then steps back and nods with his chin at the sandbars stretching out all around us. "There's a couple of these out here. My mom used to bring me here when I was little, and we'd walk up and down the shore looking for them."

We've been walking around out here for about half an hour now, starting with a slow amble down the shore toward the point, mostly talking about school—his school—and Granne.

"Oh, man, she was the scariest," he laughs, after describing some of his teachers, the OCD librarian, the sadistic soccer coach. "Sorry, I know she's your grandmother and everything, but everybody knew getting called down to Mrs. D's office was the worst."

*Oh, don't worry, I completely understand.*

"She retired at the end of my Grade 9 year, though, so we have a new principal now, Mr. MacNeill. Tries to be cool, you know? Comes out and runs with the track team, pulls out his guitar for school talent show. You know the type."

I try to picture my high school principal, Mr. Dawson, doing anything cool. It's a fail, because all I can see is him sitting with Mrs. Varma, the head of Guidance, in the little lounge area beside his office, where they met with Dad and me when I came in to school to figure out how I was going to finish my year after that thing happened. Mr. Dawson, all serious and sympathetic, but still sending out invisible waves of disapproval for messing up. I definitely like the sound of Mr. MacNeill.

We get to the end of the beach and I hear a buzz from somewhere. Casey pulls his phone out.

"Sorry," he says, eyes on screen, thumbs in action. "Beth's looking for me."

Right. Beth. The girlfriend.

Two herons have just appeared around the point and are skimming over the sandbars. They look like pterodactyls to me. Big, weird, prehistoric creatures, making their escape to Prince Edward Island.

I watch them while Casey continues to text and then I think I hear—maybe it's just that I want to hear—something behind me, and I glance up. Will took off from the café quickly this afternoon, and I didn't really talk to him much today, so just maybe …

Nothing there. Just the sand and the sandstone pebbles and small boulders at the base of the grassy point. The wildflowers and beach grass growing from the exposed red earth and the thistles sticking up everywhere. A little path that Will uses to come down to the shore—along with the local deer, porcupine, raccoons, whatever.

I look back toward the water and see that Casey is watching me. He puts his phone—and Beth—away in the pocket of his shorts.

"Hey, come on out on the sandbars. I want to show you something," he says, and that's when we venture out over the ripples of red sand toward this freshwater spring and my brave exploration of nature's mysteries.

"Were you expecting Greeny to show up?" he asks as we walk.

Not answering that one. Instead, I ask him, "Is that his nickname?"

"He's been Greeny since elementary school," Casey laughs in an *inside-joke, everybody's in on it, nobody minds* kind of way.

"Don't you have a nickname at school?"

"No, I'm not big on nicknames," I say quickly. He really doesn't need to know what people are calling me.

"He's been Greeny forever. When we all started school together, he was called Willie. Billy and Willie Greenfield. Nice, eh?"

I picture Will as a little kid starting school and decide he was probably adorable and that Willie suited him.

"So his dad has always been called Billy? Not Bill?"

"Yup. Billy. Nobody ever calls him Bill or Mr. Greenfield around here."

"Why not?"

We've now reached the farthest sandbar and Casey is searching the sand for something, feeling around with his bare foot.

"Oh, they have lots of names for Billy Greenfield, but 'Mister' isn't one of them."

He glances at me, smiling—no, he's smirking—and I can see that he really wants me to ask, so of course I don't. And that's when he finds the spring.


"I should probably get back."

My feet are cold now. The sun is dipping lower and lower,

the stars coming out. There's a slight breeze off the water and I'm glad I have my hoodie.

"Sure. Me, too," he says. Yes. Beth is waiting for him somewhere, probably tapping her toe, staring at the screen of her phone and pouting.

But we don't move right away, both of us standing there, watching the water inch toward us as the tide comes in, almost covering the freshwater spring now. It's mesmerizing. Calming, even. The darkness is moving in and with it comes a blanket of quiet. A few gulls somewhere far off, a truck on the highway on the other side of the channel. It's like everything is settling down for the night. Maybe it would be okay to stand here, watching the world go dark, for just a while longer.

And then Casey says, "Yup. There's Greeny. Checking up on us."

I turn quickly in the direction he's looking, back toward the shore.

Someone, maybe Will, is silhouetted against the sky for just a moment. I raise my arm to wave but he's already turned and is heading back over the point and out of sight.

# Rugs

"Your dad was one of the cool kids," Becca says as we pass the high school.

"No way." I'm pretty sure my mouth just dropped open. I turn away from watching the sun throwing out sparklers on the waves of the channel to stare at her.

She glances away from the road and nods at me. "Oh, yeah. He was a football star, back when the school had a football team, and he was star of the school show, playing his guitar and rocking out with Billy Greenfield and a couple of very cool brothers from over toward Linden—one of whom I dated for five years." Eyes back on the road, head nodding. "Oh, Andrew Day was cool, all right. And that's not easy when your mother is the English teacher."

Becca is driving me home from the café, because Granne is staying behind with Billy to meet with the appliance supplier to talk voltages and placement and hook-ups in the nearly completed kitchen. We're getting closer to opening, and Becca came in to do some measurements for her "rugs," as she calls them. Rugs that hang on the wall, I guess.

I'm normally kind of shy around adults I don't know, but there's something about Becca that makes me relax. Maybe because she always has this slight smile on her face, as if she's enjoying herself all the time. (Is that even possible?) And she doesn't talk a lot, which I like. It's something that Granne and I share, actually. Dad, too. Lynette not so much. The first time Dad brought Lynette home for supper, I couldn't get away from the table fast enough.

Lynette works in publishing, although not published herself. She and Dad met through some English teachers book conference about a year ago, and I guess they hit it off. She's very attractive—I don't like to think about that side of their relationship. The attraction part. She's also smart and successful at her publishing job, apparently. But oh, crap, she talks a lot.

"And then my best friend and I walked the West Coast Trail— you know what that is, right, Larkin?—and it was one of the most influential and life-changing experiences I've ever had. I can give you the link to my blog if you want."

She leans forward when she talks, leans back when she's done. As if she's trying to clear a space for herself inside her own conversation.

"Larkin, have you thought about university? Library science is a very good career path. Or straight English Lit and into publishing. I know a lot of people. Just a thought."

Dad's a little embarrassed about the whole Lynette situation, I can tell. I mean, Mom's out of the picture, obviously, but they're not officially divorced. And it's pretty clear he doesn't think Mom is ever coming back, which I understand. I don't think she's coming back, either. And I'm such great company, of course. He has to be lonely.

"So, Lynette and I are going out for supper tonight, Lark. You okay on your own?" he would ask, without making eye contact.

"Yeah, sure, Dad. No problem." Relieved I wasn't expected to go along.

Or, "Hey, Lark. Lynette's coming over to watch (insert name of Netflix British crime drama here). Want to join us?"

"No, thanks, Dad. Homework." Or talking to Amanda on my phone. Or staring at the ceiling and plugging in my ear buds and listening to music so that I can't hear them.

But Becca is completely different. She's quiet. She's calm. Her long-fingered hands lie on the steering wheel now, as if she's just resting them there, not propelling a multi-ton vehicle down the road.

She laughs a breathless, light laugh because clearly she's enjoying how stunned I am.

Stunned—Dad? *A cool kid?* But also, I'm wondering if Becca was one of the cool kids, right there with him. She must be if she dated one of his band mates for five years. I want to know but I don't want to know. It's a dilemma, and it's territory I don't really feel like exploring, so I just turn my eyes forward and shake my head. *Wow. My cool teenage dad. That's such an awkward thing to think about. Thanks for sharing that.*

We turn onto the Point road and follow the curve down between the fields that surround the Henwood farm, past the house and barn. Barns, more like. This place is huge. Silos galore. Trucks and farm vehicles everywhere, all neat and shiny and professional looking. The Henwood dairy operation is one of the biggest in the area and employs a lot of people, including Casey and his older brother, Cody (as I was informed last night during our sandbar stroll). In fact, that might be Casey on the tractor coming down the lane through that field …

I quickly look away, toward Becca and past her to the channel where the late afternoon sparklers are lighting up the waves. I don't want to wave hello at Casey like we're friends. I'm not really sure what I want to do with Casey.

But it's okay, because we're past the farm now and following the curve that straightens out between more fields, and a few small cottages, and the long lane that climbs to her house on the right, and further on, the lane to Will's house on the left, hidden by the trees. And there at the end of the road, Granne's.

Home. Nearly there. Good, because I'm tired now. Ready to be home, away, on my own.

"Would you like to come in and see the rugs I'm donating to the café?" Becca asks and takes her eyes off the road long enough to catch me in that unusual blue-gray gaze of hers. "I could use a second opinion."

And it occurs to me that if I go to Becca's for a while, I won't be home alone. Where someone might come and knock on the door and want to visit. Someone like, say, Casey, who probably just saw us drive by.

"I … sure. Sure, thanks."

"Great," she says, checking her mirror (for following tractors?) and swings up the lane toward her house, a classic two-story white farmhouse with gables in the black roof, a wide verandah overlooking the front field, over the road to another field, and the channel beyond. A bright red front door.

She parks her van in front of her garage—or maybe it's a shed—and we climb out.

"Welcome. Come on in."

It looks way too big for one person, but I don't ask. Dad said something about her being married, but she hasn't mentioned any husband in our brief conversations. I just follow her around to the back, where we enter by way of a small porch that holds two wicker chairs and a little table. The view out the back is over yet another field (yes, those Henwoods and their cows are everywhere), rising toward a distant line of trees.

"The sunrise is spectacular here," Becca says as she unlocks her door and smiles at me over her shoulder, nodding at me to follow her inside. "Feel free to come for an early cup of tea sometime. You don't get the view down at your place. Too low, and that big section of bush out behind."

I'm not sure if this is an actual invitation or just polite conversation, so I just nod, smile, don't say anything.

"Don't worry about your shoes, Larkin." She drops her keys and little leather purse on the kitchen table. I take a quick glance around at white walls, white cupboards, and shelves full of dishes and bowls and pitchers, all in a jumble of colors and sizes. Shiny metallic appliances and there, huge against one wall, an enormous black woodstove.

"In here." She leads the way and I follow her through the open doorway into the big front room. Squishy couches and chairs at one end with tables and bookshelves tucked around and behind and beside. Also, a TV against the end wall—an absolutely enormous flat-screen TV, not what I expected.

In front of the big window, overlooking the verandah and the view down over the fields to the water, there's a straight-backed wooden chair and a frame holding a stretched piece of canvas with little piles of wool strips and hunks of yarn. Scissors. Wooden-handled hooks. A small cabinet full of books and boxes. And beside the chair and frame, a set of open shelves holding wool and yarn of all colors.

Colors everywhere. On the stretched burlap canvas. All around me on the walls as I slowly look around. Hangings of all sizes, some actual images of people or trees or buildings, and some just a textured mash-up of water colors, or sky, or flowers. People dancing, an owl staring out, a horse and wagon, a giant sunflower.

"This is where I work," Becca says. "What do you think?"

I think I could work here. I could *live* here.

Back home, when Mom first went away and I was on my own a lot, Amanda's mom taught us how to knit. Squares first, then scarves, easy little baby blankets. Nothing complicated. Amanda wasn't all that interested but I was. The clicking of the needles was soothing, but it was the yarn—especially the good stuff, hand-dyed and textured and unpredictable. Dad would take me to the big craft store and I'd stock up on different colors and thicknesses, and then I'd knit them into blankets and scarves and donate them to the church down the street. Or the humane society for their unclaimed cats. He took me out to a couple of craft shows, where artsy people who live on alpaca farms would have these bins of incredible yarn—"fiber, dear," said one older lady, her gray hair in kindergarten pigtails—and Dad bought me a pile. Most of it still in my closet at home because, shortly after starting junior high, things changed so much, got complicated.

And then I got to high school—and forget it.

But now, standing here in Becca's front room, I'm remembering.

"It's—this is—I don't know," I say finally and she laughs.

"I know."

I look at her then. She's smiling at me and I think maybe she does know.

"My yarn stash is ridiculous," she says, nodding toward the shelves.

I think her yarn stash is beautiful, and my face must be saying that because she laughs again.

"I think you're one of us, Larkin. I can see it ... am I right?"

"Well, I do know how to knit," I say, shrug. No need to go into any details about Amanda and me at the kitchen table, and her mother guiding the yarn through our fingers so that we'd be holding it just right, for just the perfect tension. Needles clunky at first, then smooth. The rhythm of it. Amanda never really got the rhythm of knitting, but I did.

"I knew it." Becca steps over to the shelves and reaches out for a skein (See? I know the lingo, too) of something fuzzy in a rich swirl of blue-green.

Actually, she takes two skeins and then holds them out to me.

"Here. Hand-dyed merino, from the sheep farm over near River John," she says. "Make a scarf. You'll never feel the chill again, I promise."

But I hesitate. This stuff is really expensive, I remember. "Oh, I couldn't …"

"Yes, you could," says Becca, depositing the two skeins in the crook of my elbow where I cradle them so they don't drop. She turns to a cabinet, pulls a drawer open, and rummages around, coming up with a package. Knitting needles. Wooden and fairly large. "Here. Perfect. Just cast on about twenty stitches and knit every row until you run out. It'll be gorgeous."

"Thank you," I manage to say, because I feel a bit like I'm underwater and she just threw me a line. A gorgeous, blue-green, hand-dyed line from the sheep farm over near River John.

"I have a spinner, but do you know how to wind the skein on the back of a chair?"

I nod—that's something Amanda's mom showed me. My fingers are submerged in the skeins, like they're swimming. I can't wait to get back to my own room and unravel the skein, throw it over the back of a chair, and wind the yarn into a ball.

"Thanks," I say again, but she just laughs.

"I recognize a fellow traveler when I see one," she says. "Now, what about the rugs?"

She points at one of the rugs hanging on the wall behind me and nods for me to look, too.

"What do you think of this one? Think it will look good there between the Mystery and Romance sections?"

Bookshelves full of books. Only it's a rug. It's also huge, almost life-size. I step toward it and peer closely at the bumpy texture of the fiber loops. Tiny loops like pixels. When I'm close up, I can't see the image, but when I step back ...

"It's perfect."

"I think so, too."

I turn and smile at her. "It's absolutely perfect."

"Great." Becca rubs her hands together. "I'm so pleased you agree."

She steps closer and reaches out with one hand to touch the bumpy swirls of wool, as if she's stroking a cat.

"I'll miss this one. But I can visit it any time—at the café, right? And I know it's a favorite of Anne's."

I picture it there, on the wall where it will be the first thing anyone sees when they come in the door. Books among the books.

"Maybe I'll take it in tonight," Becca says, dropping her hand but still looking at it. "I know Billy's going to be there, working late. He could help me hang it, and it would be there for Anne to see first thing tomorrow when she comes in."

A moment of silence and I take a quick glance at her. *Goodbye.* That's what the expression on her face says.

She turns and catches my eye, shrugs.

"Now, a cup of tea, lots more chat about your cool dad, and then I'll take you home so you can start that scarf. Sound good?"

She's already heading back to the kitchen, so I don't need to say anything. Which is good, because I really hope she's kidding about the cool dad part.

## Her voice

I'm walking really fast, almost running, across the sand and pebbles, broken shells, seaweed dried into nests, and then over the cool, rippled sand. Splash into the waves that are inching out, leaving the sandbars emerging as islands now.

I'm out of breath but being out of breath is good, because I'm sure if I could breathe, I would also be yelling at the world to just stop. I'm already crying and there just isn't enough breath to go around.

Dad called right as Granne and I settled down on the deck after supper. I've brought out my knitting needles and Becca's merino yarn, which I wound into a ball as soon as I got home. Yes, Granne has wine. No, I do not.

"Hey, Lark," he says and we exchange the usual lies about how good we're doing. Then he coughs and says, "Someone here wants to talk to you."

I'm still preparing myself for the conversation we're going to have about that night at the bonfire and my introduction to the local social scene because, of course, Granne would have reported to him. But no, that's not where he goes. I hear him handing over the phone, saying, "Here she is." Then someone breathing.

No. No, Dad …

"Larkin? Is that you? Is that my baby Lark?"

I can't believe it. He's making me talk to my mother.

"Hi." It takes me two tries to say it because my mouth and throat are suddenly dry. I stand up quickly—Granne actually jumps as the knitting needles fall to the deck—and I head for the steps down to the yard. I don't want to do this in front of her, so I just keep striding across the grass and down toward the shore. "Hi, Mom."

"Hi, honey. It's so good to hear your voice."

It's not great to hear her voice. She sounds shaky. Or sleepy or something. In my head, I'm shrieking at my dad, *Are you kidding me? Why are you doing this?*

"So … how's your … how's your summer going there, Lark—out there with your … your grandmother?"

"Good. It's good."

Pause. The sound of her breathing, maybe a low hum as she's thinking. Then, "And ... and are you having fun? Are you ... are you meeting people? Meeting ... kids?"

"Yeah. I've met some kids here on the Point." Casey (don't quite trust him). Beth (stink eye, hates me). Will (appears to be keeping his distance). Oh, yes, I'm doing well in that department.

"So it's good? It's ... good, then?"

"Oh, yeah, all good."

In other words, I lie.

And it doesn't matter because I can tell, she's either medicated or exhausted into confusion and not really taking in what I'm saying.

"Good, good. Well ..." (long pause, labored breath, moan) "... bye, now, honey. Love you. Bye. Here's ... here's Dad. Love you, Lark ... my Larkin ..."

I hear the phone being fumbled and handed over, and that's when I hang up, power off, and walk out as far as I can go, until I'm finally standing on the edge of the last sandbar, one step from launching myself and perhaps my phone toward Prince Edward Island.

Breathing, crying, trying not to hear her voice because it's not the voice I remember.

I'm spinning around like the inside of a washing machine, over and around, metal screeching and buckling around us. She's screaming my name.

I remember that the most. *Larkin—Larkin!* My mother screaming my name from the front seat.

And then lying in the hospital with my neck encased in some torture device. I know now it was a neck brace and that they were worried about my spine, but it just feels like torture and I'm crying for my mother, my father.

Dad's there, pressing his hands to the sides of my head, wiping tears away from my face and looking into my eyes and saying over and over, "It's okay, Lark. You're going to be okay. I'm here, Mom's here, you're going to be fine. You're safe."

I don't feel safe. For the first time in my life, I don't feel safe.

I'm six years old.

It's a while later that I find out that Mom's back is hurt, not broken or anything like that, but she'll have to have an operation. The doctors and nurses smile at me when they tell me, with Dad there holding my hand, so I think it's okay to not be afraid. It's going to be all right.

And, at first, it is all right. It's only later, slowly, we find out that it isn't.

"Hey."

I jump and turn around to see Will walking toward me. *How long have I been standing here, staring out at the tide?*

I turn away quickly because I don't want him to see my face, which I'm sure is streaked with tears.

"Hey."

He comes up beside me—not right beside me, but there, on the island sandbar—and we stand in silence for a few moments. My breathing starts to slow down and I think maybe I'm coming back to myself. Which is good, because he's already seen me freak out once, and he really doesn't need to see how often this happens to me.

"I thought for a minute there, maybe you were gonna go for a swim," he says.

Yeah, maybe that's what it looked like to him as I flew across the sand, kicking up water, trying to get away from her voice. And he's right, of course, because I was thinking that—thinking about going for a long swim. Not for the first time, either.

"Sometimes," I just go for it. "Sometimes I think I could just walk into the water and start swimming toward Prince Edward Island. But I would never ever get there, right?"

He doesn't freak out or anything. He stands there as if he's seriously considering my question.

"The tide would probably get you," he says finally. "Currents. You'd end up somewhere else."

"Somewhere else. Like somewhere dead? Drowned?"

"No … somewhere else, like River John," he says, and now I turn and look at him. He's squinting a bit, as if he's calculating distances on some mental map. "Or maybe Seafoam. You'd just have to keep your head above water and you'd be okay, probably."

"What … there's actually a place called Seafoam?"

He nods, grins at me. "There is."

"Seafoam." I'd be okay ending up in a place called Seafoam.

"Hey, I was wondering if you want to take our kayaks out," he says. "Tide's still coming in, so we'd have to drag them over the sand, but the channel's good all the way out to the reef and no boats are out tonight. It's nice on the water this time of night."

I've never kayaked before, but it's a step up from swimming. And Will would be there in case I flipped myself into the water.

And it would be quiet, and—away.

"I need to let Granne know."

"Sure. Got your phone, right?"

He must have been out here already when I came running down, talking to my mother.

But I'm not sure I want to turn it on and see the fifty messages and missed calls from Dad. I do anyway.

Yup. Five texts and three missed calls. Ignore.

She answers on the first ring. She's probably standing in the kitchen, watching us out the window. I bet Dad called her, too.

"Granne? Yeah, I'm with Will. We're thinking of taking his kayaks out."

"Lovely night for it. Wear a life jacket."

"Yup, okay. See you later."

"Straight home after … right, Larkin?"

"Okay." We sign off and I nod at Will, waiting and watching.

"All good."

"Great, let's go."

We start back over the sandbars and I make sure my phone is turned off.

# Kayaks

He didn't tell me that I'd be getting wet. The kayaks are like big boards that we sit on—on, rather than in—and propel ourselves over the water with a double-bladed paddle.

"My dad calls them 'flotation devices' rather than kayaks," he tells me and I can see why, since we're just sitting on top of these heavy plastic boards with carved-out seats and foot rests. And they really are heavy, too, as I discovered while hauling mine across the sand in front of his place, so we could launch into the channel. "But they're great for paddling along the shore. I wouldn't want to go across the Strait or anything too far, though."

So no trips to Seafoam tonight, I guess.

He paddles with the smooth, rhythmic stroke of someone who's done this before.

When I paddle, I bring a spray of water flying up and over my legs—my still-bruised and not-yet-transformed-by-the-summer-sun legs. My shoulders are already feeling the strain and I'm pretty sure I have a blister starting on my right thumb. In other words, I'm showing off what a complete beach and water rookie I am. And Will pulls far ahead of me right from the start.

But it's still good, because the sun is just thinking about setting and the stars are coming out and the water is smooth and calm, and I'm starting to feel like I can breathe again after hearing my mother's voice.

My mother's voice.

It was just a shock, that's all. I wish Dad had warned me first. It's been so long since I've heard her speak. Maybe last December, during my grandparents' Christmas Day call? No, longer ago than that. Last summer's duty visit ...

"You okay?" Will asks.

I'm drifting. Apparently I can't think and paddle at the same time.

He turns around and glides back toward me, resting his paddle across his thighs. Beyond him, the sky is starting to layer into those sunset streaks of orange and pink and lilac, and the water stretches all satiny and dark blue out into the Strait. He could be a painting: *Boy on water at sunset.*

No, *Boy being nice to messed-up girl on water at sunset.*

"Yeah."

He watches me for a moment, which is unnerving, and then says, "You sure?"

I wonder what he sees. Maybe the fading bruise around my eye, the bruises on my thighs. Maybe there's something about the way my eyes are still shiny with tears, or that I have my mouth clamped shut so that my lips won't shake.

Oh, hell, why not.

"I talked to my mother tonight," I tell him. "That's why I was booking it out on the shore. It wasn't great, because she's in a rehab place out in Vancouver for her addiction to drugs. Mostly painkillers. She gets out sometimes and everybody thinks she's going to be okay, and then she disappears and turns up in hospital again. Or the police find her and bring her in."

I can't stop myself and it feels awful, not like relieving the pressure or *you'll feel better if you talk to someone, Larkin,* like the counselor keeps saying, but more like stabbing myself in the head with every word. No, wait—it feels more like non-stop puking, as if the words are erupting from inside me and spewing all over, making a mess.

"She's tried suicide a few times, too, but somebody always finds her and brings her back. I haven't seen her for a few years. My dad and I would go out to visit in the summer. Stay with my grandparents and visit her at the facility, or, one year, she was staying at the house."

"Jesus," says Will. I know he's watching me but I'm just looking up at the sky. It's so much easier to talk to the sky than to this guy, who now has one hand on the edge of my kayak so that I don't drift away.

"And I was supposed to be going with my dad this summer because she's just recovering from another episode, but I couldn't go because this thing happened—this thing happened at school, and I messed up so much that Dad thought maybe it would be bad for everyone, so I came here, instead."

Talk about spewing. And just like after a big burst of puking, I'm now completely empty and exhausted. My hands are clenched around the paddle, but I couldn't make it work right now if my life depended on it.

So instead, I gaze up into the gradually darkening sky as the stars start to emerge and we just drift.

"Jesus," he says again.

There's nothing more to say. We drift some more until I can't stand the silence.

"Yeah. Whatever. Let's just paddle."

So we do. Turn out toward the reef and paddle away from me and my drama.

Now I wish I hadn't said anything because it's so awkward when you download your crap on someone and they don't know what to say. Will is paddling kind of lightly, keeping his kayak right beside mine, and I bet he's wishing he'd never asked me on this little adventure. He's probably wondering why he even spoke to me that first night on the shore, why he gave me that advice about being careful around Casey and Beth.

"My dad used to drink a lot," he says suddenly. We both stop paddling. "I know it's different, but I kind of get it. You and your mom, I mean."

"Used to?"

"Yeah, he cleaned himself up after he burned down a shed he was building at the Henwoods' about ten years ago."

"He burned down a shed? Like, on purpose?"

"Nah. Dropped a burning cigarette, got distracted and busy and didn't notice, and it caught." His eyes are on the reef ahead of us, rising like a spine above the tide. "At least, that's the story. He couldn't remember."

"Yikes. Well, it's good that he's cleaned himself up, right?"

He shrugs. "Yeah. But nobody ever forgets stuff like that around here."

Ah. Lightbulb moment. Casey saying, *Nobody calls him Mr. Greenfield.*

"Do you ever think—ever wonder—ever worry that maybe one day you'll be, you know, like him?" I think about the bonfire and I'm pretty sure, as I squint back through my hazy memories, that Will didn't have anything to drink.

"No. Never. At least, not the drinking part." And then he looks at me. "Do you? Worry about being like your mom, I mean?"

The big question. She got hooked on painkillers after the accident, we know that. And it just grew and grew as she added on other treats, like booze, like other pills. What if that need was there all along? Who knows? And what if that need is inside me, too? What if that need is the reason I now see the fading evidence of my last bad choice on my face in the mirror every day?

"I don't know."

Another few moments of drifting, and then:

"Seals," he points toward the reef where silvery-black lumps lie in groups along the ridge. Lumps that appear to have faces.

A few of them slide off into the water, raising a huge splash. Then their heads break the surface and they look around, bobbing, see us, dip below the waves, and disappear.

Which gives me the creepy feeling that creatures of the deep will be circling underneath us, like sharks maybe, ready to leap out of the water and land on our boards. Or maybe dump us into the water. And eat us.

Okay, Larkin, enough.

"They're not—not violent, are they?"

Will laughs. "No way. They're like dogs. Just curious." He turns and grins at me. "Casey and I used to swim with them when we were kids. It was great."

I picture two little-boy versions of Casey and Will, hanging out, getting into trouble. Is Will even capable of getting into trouble?

"So I guess you've known Casey forever?"

"Forever. We started school together. Played Timbits hockey, soccer. Baseball. Bible camp." At that, he turns and gives a shrug. "It's a thing around here."

"No, don't worry. I have my little secrets, too." Sparks. Brownies.

The year Amanda and I enrolled in a hip-hop dance class. Those little-kid moments, boxed up and stored away so no one can see them, thank goodness.

"Yeah, I guess it was a Point thing. Henny and Greeny." He laughs. "We were well known."

"Henny?" I can't help smiling at that. Casey, the cool kid— Henny?

"His name. Henwood—easy to shorten, and with the farm. Chickens, you know?" Will says. "I don't think anyone calls him that anymore, though."

"But you're still Greeny."

"Yeah. Only to him. He's the only one who calls me that." And now he's not laughing, just looking off over the water. "Because, of course, what do you think of when you hear the word *greeny*?" Now he turns to me. "Snot, right?"

"Well, I wasn't going to say it, but yes. Snot."

"Yeah. Greeny. Just a little reminder between Point kids who go way back."

"Reminder?"

"That he's a Henwood and I'm not."

Got it.

At that moment, the rest of the seals launch themselves into the water with much splashing, and I see that the reef has almost disappeared under the tide. Some of the sandbars, too. Yay. This means we'll be able to get closer to shore when we take the kayaks back.

And it's probably time, too. The sun is just about to set and the bright pastels along the horizon have darkened, along with the shades of blue overhead. Stars are out.

"Ready to go back?" he asks and I nod.

We turn our kayaks—his turn is all smooth and effortless, mine is completed with a lot of clunking and splashing—and we head back toward the Point.

"You're okay now, eh, Larkin?" he asks.

"Yeah." For now, anyway. "Thanks."

"Good." A beat, then: "Race you!"

Total fail, but at least it makes me laugh.

# When you get a phone call in the middle of the night

The ringing of the phone in the kitchen wakes me. Three times, then it stops. I can hear Granne's voice from her room down the hall—she must have answered it there.

It's dark. I roll over and pull the quilt up. The wind has come up and it's floating my curtains around a bit, so there's motion and sound, and I just want to block it all out.

Then Granne's door opens loudly and she's heading to the bathroom. Is she sick?

I roll over on my back and listen. Tap turned on. A minute later the toilet flushes. The door opens and now she's in the kitchen. A crack of light under my door.

I slip out of bed and grab my hoodie, because the room feels cold with the breeze pouring in through the window. Open my door and see the light on in the kitchen.

It's dark, still middle-of-the-night dark.

I stand in the kitchen doorway and squint at Granne.

"Oh, Larkin, I was just leaving you a note," she says as she straightens up from the kitchen table. I see a few words written on the message pad in front of her.

"What's going on?" I ask, and I'm afraid because Granne's face is unfamiliar, white, all the lines around her eyes and mouth drawing down and her eyes wide with—something. Something I've never seen in her face. Always in control, always calm. But now her mouth is set, hard, and her hand is shaking as she puts down her pen.

"I have to get into town. There's a fire."

"A fire? Where?" Why does Granne have to go to a fire in the middle of night? Fuzzy brain.

"The café is on fire, Larkin. I'm going, now."

"I'll come with you. Give me a sec."

I head back to my room and switch on the light. No way I'm hanging out here by myself while she's in town watching the café burn.

"I'll be in the car," she calls to me. "Hurry."

The road is transformed in the dark. The headlights pick up the daisies and tiger lilies and tall grass in the ditches, all waving in the wind and acting weirdly, like creatures bowing and dancing as we drive by.

"Who called to tell you?"

"John Clarke. Volunteer firefighter."

Her words are short and monotone. She has both hands on the wheel and is clearly not in the mood to chat. We pass Becca's house, all dark. I picture her beautiful rug, the one with the books—*Maybe I'll take it in tonight. It would be there for Anne to see first thing tomorrow when she comes in*—and then we're cruising around the curve faster than is probably wise. My right hand goes smack against the door to hold me steady.

"Sorry," Granne says.

"It's okay."

Past the Henwood farm with its numerous outside lights throwing shadows around the huge barnyard.

I glance at the clock: 3:35.

Granne ignores the stop sign at the end of the road and just keeps going, speeding up on to the main road toward town.

*My grandmother just broke the law*, I think. And that's when I smell the smoke and hear sirens in the distance.

# The books

He picks it up on the first ring. I bet he's been carrying it around all night, staring at it, willing my name to flash up on the screen.

"Lark! Are you okay? I'm so sorry …"

"Dad, it's okay," I cut him off. "I'm not calling about that. It's—it's just—there's a fire."

I know I'm in that weird place where my brain is all jumbled up, so I close my eyes to try to force the words to come out in order, try to understand the words coming at me now from my dad, panicking out there on the West Coast.

"Lark! The house is on fire? Are you safe? Where are you?"

"No, no. Not the house. It's the café, Granne's café."

"You're—wait, you're at the café? There's a fire at the café? Are you safe, Larkin? Is Granne with you? Is she okay?"

*Geez, Dad, please stop rattling off the questions. I can't answer them all.*

I don't say that out loud, but even just thinking it helps me focus.

"Dad, listen. We got a phone call that there was a fire at the café, so Granne and I just drove in and the firefighters are here. It's okay, we're okay, but there's lots of smoke and there were some flames toward the back. But it's okay at the front."

Yeah, now I'm rambling.

"Where are you?"

"I'm sitting on the steps of the post office, across the street."

"Good girl. Good. And Granne?"

"She's over there with the firefighters. They told her to stay here but she just went anyway. She's talking to one of them. I can see her."

She's standing there with her arms tightly folded—no, more like tightly wrapped around herself—talking with a man in a helmet and heavy yellow jacket. Firefighter gear. Four or five other guys dressed the same have been moving around the side and back of the café, where the smoke is, hauling a hose from one of the trucks pulled up to one side. The engine or some part of the truck's equipment (what do I know about fire trucks? Nothing.) rumbles over every other sound.

It's the lights, though, that are the worst part. Flashing red and blue lights split the darkness over and over and over. Like someone tapping hard on my forehead and saying *danger, danger, danger*. The lights flash on Granne so that she's lit up, then in shadow, lit up, in shadow again.

"I can see her," I tell my dad.

"Are you alone there, Lark? Are you okay?"

He's afraid I'm going to have one of my famous freak-out sessions, but the funny thing is, I know I'm not going to. Maybe it's Granne, seeing her like that—her face all white and stretched downward—that makes me tuck up inside myself, ready to help her.

Or maybe I'm just too tired to react and it will all hit me later. Yeah, that's probably it.

"Don't worry about me, Dad. I'm okay. I'm just waiting for Granne to come back and tell me what's happening."

But I don't need her to tell me. I can see it with my own eyes. I know where all the rooms are, the kitchen, the storage room with the books. That's where the flames were when we arrived— pouring out of the storage room window.

Yup, those books are toast.

"As long as you and Granne are safe, Lark, that's the important thing." He sounds awful—is he *crying*?

"We're okay. How are you?"

Long pause. I hear him cough, sniff. "I'm okay, too, but it's been a day here. Lark, I'm so sorry about that call earlier."

"Yeah. It's okay, Dad. I'm sorry I hung up on you." How to explain it? I probably don't have to. He knows.

"She asked. Out of nowhere. She just asked and I just didn't want to say no."

"Yeah, it's okay."

There's a long pause, because neither of us knows what to say next, and neither of us wants to hang up. I spend this gap watching Granne, who turns around to see if I'm still in position on the steps. She doesn't unwrap her arms from around herself, though. She just takes a long look over at me and then turns back to watching her dream go up in smoke.

# Plans

The phone keeps ringing and ringing, waking me up over and over as I drift in and out of the light. And it's light, all right. It was already light when we got back from the fire and I followed Granne up the steps of the deck into the kitchen.

"Get some sleep, Larkin," she says, kind of like an order, actually. "Or do you want something to eat first?"

"No, thanks." I don't want food, or drink, or anything except sleep.

Actually, it's not sleep I want—I just want to be unconscious. I want to blot out the sound of those trucks, and the firefighters' voices calling out instructions and reporting on damage, and the hiss of water from the high-pressure hose directed at the back of the café.

And Granne's silence as we finally got back to the car and she drove us home.

Yeah, I just want to roll myself in my quilt and disappear into my own silence for a while. So, no food. No anything.

Except the freaking phone, which keeps ringing me awake, followed by Granne's voice. I can't hear what she says, just that she's talking. People must be calling to see what happened and to check up on her. Which is nice, of course, but I wish she'd adjust the ringer or something so I can't hear it. Even better, why doesn't she get her own cell phone like everyone else in this century?

Okay, I give up. The old-school clock radio beside my bed shows that it's just after noon, which means I got about four hours of sleep once I left Granne plugging in the kettle when we got home from the fire. Four hours of phone-disturbed sleep, that is. I roll onto my back and let the quilt fall away. Stare at the ceiling and tune my ears to Granne's voice, out there in the kitchen. Talking on the phone.

"I'll tell her. Thank you for calling, Casey," she says.

Casey Henwood calling me?

Will and his dad both showed up at the café at some point in the early hours, as it was just getting light and everything was wrapping up. Fire out. No more smoke. Firefighters packing up some equipment, but continuing to stomp in and out of the building (which looked perfectly okay from the front, weirdly) or stand around talking, to each other and to Granne, who never left her station on the sidewalk. Of course, by then I was almost horizontal with tiredness on the Post Office steps across the street. I saw Will look over at me, wave once in greeting, but then he turned back to Granne. Sticking close to Billy, who was hunched over and jittery and chain smoking.

All their hard work. Just like the books.

They stand there with Granne for a while and talk to her and some of the firefighters, then they turn back to their truck.

But first Will makes a quick detour to the Post Office and me.

"Do you want a ride home, or …?" His hair is sticking out from under his ball cap, as if he put it on in a hurry. Shadows on his jaw where his morning stubble has sprouted. He stands there, swinging his keys, and lets his words trail off, looking at me and probably noticing that I'm not at my best. But, hey, neither is he.

"No, thanks. I'll wait for Granne." I can hardly get the words out, I'm feeling so groggy now, but he just nods, gives me a tight little smile, and turns to follow his dad to their truck. I notice that he's driving. Maybe Billy's too shaken up, thinking about all his work gone to waste.

A few spectators come out to see the show, but Casey Henwood isn't one of them. Word travels fast, though.

But now it's the morning after. When I get to the kitchen, Granne is drinking coffee, sitting at the table with her computer fired up and a pile of file folders spread around. She takes a quick look at me—giving me her "Is Larkin okay?" look. Apparently I pass inspection.

"Sorry about the phone. I'm sure you didn't get much sleep, did you?"

"No, but it's okay."

"There's coffee if you want some. Or put the kettle on."

"Okay. I'm not really hungry yet."

She glances over at me and leans back in her chair. "No, I understand. That wasn't a fun experience, was it?"

Worse for her, of course. But she seems to be back to familiar principal-in-charge Mrs. D this morning.

"What are you doing?" I nod at her workstation.

"Just making a spreadsheet of repairs and next steps," she

says and turns back to her screen. "No time to waste if we want to open this month."

Wow. Go, Granne. "Really? Do you think everything can be fixed up that fast?"

Now she leans back and looks at me with her teacher look. "Yes, everything can be fixed up that fast. The fire was contained to the kitchen area and the storage room at the back, and the fire crew did a great job of getting it under control quickly and blowing out the worst of the smoke. Billy and Will can replace the drywall and flooring and rebuild the kitchen framework and the wall to the storage room." Her eyes go back to her spreadsheet, and she's now talking and typing at the same time. "Fortunately, the cabinet doors and the appliances weren't installed yet. And the countertop was temporary, anyway, with the new one coming with the cabinet doors. So a big cleanup and installation there."

"Yes, but …" It was a fire. Flames, smoke, damage. But she's acting as if it's a minor setback.

"Yes, but what?" She glances at me again, and I have an idea of what it must have been like to be a teacher on her staff. *What do you mean you can't mark those exams and have your grades submitted by this afternoon? Nonsense!*

"I saw flames," I say. "And smoke. And those hoses. Wasn't there a lot of damage? Like, doesn't that all have to be cleaned up and inspected and everything?"

"Oh, it will be," she says, eyes back on her computer for a minute, then: "Of course, the worst part was losing the storage room and that dividing wall. The fire marshal said that's where it started, along the wall. Maybe electrical, but we'll have the wiring checked and reinstalled, which will slow reconstruction down a bit." She pauses. "And, of course, we lost all the books."

She looks at me then because, I don't know, maybe she thinks I'm going to be sad about this?

"Yeah, all those books."

"Yes, all those books, unfortunately, after so many kind donations." Eyes back on her screen. "But no worries. We'll just have to dig up some more. I've already phoned around to all my teacher friends and librarians, and they've got it going out on the forums all up and down the county. Becca even designed a poster."

While I'm trying to get over the shock of Granne knowing about forums, she brings up a screen on her computer and waves me over to look.

*"Post-Fire Book Donations Needed! Help the new Tuttle Harbour Café and Reading Room fill its shelves!"* And then details about drop-off points and people to call.

And in the background, the image of Becca's rug with the bookshelves.

I'd forgotten about Becca's rug.

"Oh, no. Becca's rug," I breathe, and stop, because the idea of that beautiful piece of art being smoked into the ashes of that dividing wall actually hurts.

Granne waves it off, though. "Not to worry. Becca called this morning to see how she could help. The rug is still safely at her house."

Well, that explains some of the phone calls, at least.

"Oh, yes," she says, eyes back on her screen. "And Casey Henwood also called to say some of the local kids are meeting at the back shore for a swim this afternoon, and you would be very welcome. If you're interested."

Casey Henwood and the back shore do not call up good memories for me. I wonder if Will is going.

"Okay. Maybe."

"Or … I'm heading into the café to meet up with Billy and

draw up our plan of attack," Granne says. "You're welcome to join us."

Granne, Billy, and the smoke-damaged café, or the back shore with the locals.

"I'll stay here," I say. "Maybe I'll go around the shore. Not sure. I'm pretty tired."

She doesn't look my way or lift her hands off the keyboard.

"Take care of yourself," she says, which makes me think of Will again. "But it is a lovely day for a swim, after all. You do what you like."

She's telling me she trusts me, and that's something.

"Okay."

Okay. I'll think about it.

# Word on the street

I don't go around the shore for a swim. Instead I go back under my quilt.

Granne sticks her head in before leaving for town, checking up on me. I pretend to be asleep but she speaks anyway. You can't fool a grandmother, I guess.

"You need to get moving at some point, Larkin. I left egg salad in the fridge for you to make a sandwich, and there are fresh strawberries, too. Also apples. Get some fresh air. I'll be back around four."

She ducks out again, closing the door behind her without waiting for my reply. Pretty sure she knows I heard every word.

Actually, I'm starving. I take a quick shower first, because I swear I can smell smoke in my hair, and then I find clean clothes, make my sandwich, and take it out on the deck, where I eat it with my feet up on the railing. And when I'm done, I go back inside for my knitting and bring it out, so I can feel the sun on my face and hear the water while I knit row after mindless row with Becca's yarn. Take breaks to look at the gulls hanging out down on the sandbars, being all chill in the sun.

Every now and then I hear shouts, voices on the wind. Action at the back shore where Casey and the gang are swimming.

Yeah, Casey and the gang don't need to see me in a bathing suit. Most of the bruises have faded but, yeah. No.

Bruises. I haven't thought about them for a while. Of course, I avoid looking in mirrors, which helps. But I know there are still tinges of green around my eye, some yellow along my jaw. And nobody needs to see the nice pastels on my upper arms, my thighs. A bathing suit would be a very bad idea.

This is good here on the deck, alone, with the breeze drying my hair into a frizzy mess and the sun on my face. I pull up the legs of my yoga pants so my knees at least get some sun, too, peel off my hoodie so my arms are exposed. Close my eyes, lean back, let the knitting needles lie in my lap, and turn my face up to the sky… and just let it go. *Count. Breathe. Let it all go*, like that mindfulness counselor said. All that stuff back home. My mother's voice. The smoky smell of burning books.

The sun and breeze are warm, gentle, soothing, even. Maybe I'll go back to sleep out here ...

"Hi, Larkin."

Maybe not, because my heart just did a complete 360 in my chest as I jerk awake in my chair. Grab my hoodie, which sends the yarn and needles clattering to the deck, roll down my yoga pants. Cover myself from—from what?

It's Chelsea, standing below the deck, smiling up at me. Bathing suit under her T-shirt and jean shorts, and a little pack slung over her shoulder with a towel. She's wearing a ball cap (logo of well-known beer) with her two bottle-enhanced red braids sticking out underneath. On her way to the beach? On her way back?

"I'm so sorry!" she says, as I scramble to find the appropriate words to use when someone has just appeared out of nowhere and scared the shit out of you. "I didn't mean to wake you up. Sorry!"

"It's okay." There, that works. "I wasn't asleep. Just, kind of ... relaxing. Long night last night."

"Oh, I know and I'm so sorry," she says, making the sympathetic face that people make in situations like this. You know, when someone's been up all night watching their grandmother's pet project spew flames and smoke into the sky. "I just wondered if you wanted to go for a swim. Some of us are meeting up over at Henwoods' beach." She nods her head in the direction of the back shore. "We could walk around together, if you want. I was just coming up the road and saw Mrs. D driving out, so I figured you might be here on your own and looking for some company."

She's one of those girls who sends out friendly vibes. I remember talking to her briefly on that mostly hazy and forgettable night at the bonfire about a TV show we both liked, and how she tried to persuade stink-eye Beth that it was worth watching. How she and Will complained about their bosses to each other—his at the Co-op (not Granne), hers at the bakery. I thought she was nice. Until I got to the point where I wasn't thinking anymore, of course. Which she would have witnessed along with all the rest of them.

I haven't seen her since then, so it's a bit awkward now. Because I really don't want to go to the back shore for a swim, but I don't want to hurt her feelings, either, when she's just being nice and including me.

"I'm actually really tired," I say. Not a lie, so it's easy to look pathetic and exhausted because I am. "I think I'm just going to stay here and take it easy this afternoon." I wave one hand at the pile of knitting under my chair.

She nods. "No problem. Just thought with Mrs. D gone, you might be lonely."

"Thanks. No, I'm not lonely. But thanks for stopping by. And have a nice time over there." I nod vaguely over my shoulder. "Casey called to invite me, too, but I just think I'll stay close to home today, if you guys don't mind."

"Totally get that," Chelsea smiles up at me. "Casey just probably wants to hear all about the fire, anyway. You know, he's the worst gossip ever." She laughs. *Oh, that Casey!* "Oh, and Will probably won't be there, right? If that's what you're worried about?" She nods at me meaningfully as she says this.

I have no idea what is meaningful about it. "Will?"

"Well, yeah. Casey says Will is probably staying close to home because it was his dad's smoking that started the fire, right? And Will probably feels terrible about it. Poor Will."

There's a buzz in the air and it's coming from nowhere.

Wait, maybe it's coming from inside my head. I try to say something simple like, *Oh, really? Is that what Casey says?*

"You didn't know, did you?" Chelsea grimaces, apologizing again. "I'm so sorry. I thought you would have heard."

Heard? From where? I've been stranded in the dark on the Post Office steps or under a quilt for the past twelve hours.

I shake my head, no.

*Billy, all tense and huddled up as he stood with Granne last night. Billy, chain smoking as he watched the café burn.*

"I'm sure Will feels terrible," she says again.

"Yeah." I don't even know what to say because it's too much to process. The buzzing is growing louder in my head and there are pin pricks of light around the edges of my vision, and I know that within the next few minutes, I'm going to have to end this conversation and find a safe, quiet place to breathe and count and all that. Granne isn't here to run after me and bring me home.

"Oh, sorry, but I think I hear the phone," I stand quickly, teetering, nearly knocking my chair over, and Chelsea looks through the railing at me in surprise. No phone ringing anywhere and she knows it. I lean down and scrabble with my hands to retrieve the knitting. "Have a nice time. See you." I force my legs to move, force my feet to carry me across the deck.

"Oh, okay," she says. Then: "Larkin—are you all right?"

"Yup! Absolutely! Bye!" Send this over my shoulder as I stuff the needles and yarn into their little bag, reach for the sliding door, and open it carefully so I can finally step through the magic portal that will take me to the safety of the kitchen, the hallway, my room.

"Bye!" I don't glance back at Chelsea as I wave and slide the door closed behind me, because I don't want to see her standing there confused and wondering what the hell is wrong with Larkin Day, the messed-up girl.

# Visitors

After that thing happened back home with Jonah and all the crap that followed, I spent a lot of time in my room, wrapped up in my duvet with the blinds pulled shut, listening to Lynette telling Dad that he needed to get me out of there and sit me down and talk to me.

Dad didn't do that. He'd crack the door open and look at me, probably just long enough to convince himself that I was still breathing, and then he'd close the door. During those first few days, he'd slip in with some juice or a snack and sit on the edge of my bed without talking. He'd just reach out with one hand and rub my back, or shoulder, or head, whatever lump he landed on, firm and gentle at the same time.

It was perfect, because I knew he was there and he knew I was there.

And after a while, I was able to push away the duvet and roll on my back and look at him. The first thing he did was smile at me.

"You know I love you, don't you, Larkin?"

Which made me cry, of course. He might have cried, too. But it was okay.

And after that we made a plan. Get through exams. Make arrangements with Granne. Do what we have to do. Stick together, even if we're at opposite ends of the country. Okay, not an easy plan but something, at least.

Granne had a plan, too. She's out in the kitchen right now, talking with Billy and Will, who showed up at the kitchen door just after supper, and it feels like the plan is just getting more and more complicated.

I had managed to eat our supper of homemade macaroni ("comfort food," she called it), to act somewhat normal, although I'm sure Granne could tell something was up. And I couldn't tell her. What could I say? That Chelsea heard from Casey that it was Billy who started the fire?

I know all about the "what people are saying" part. I know that some of it is true and most of it isn't.

But still ...

Billy and his cigarettes.

The story Will told me about the Henwood shed all those years ago.

People talking.

*Larkin says Jonah … well, you know what. At Anil's party. But of course she was drunk.*

*I heard stoned AND drunk. She's so messed up.*

*Just like her mother, right?*

*Yeah, no surprise. And Jonah says she was the one acting weird and she jumped out of his car while it was moving. That's where the bruises came from. Not from anything he did.*

*Yeah, but he's kind of a jerk, too. She might be telling the truth.*

*Who knows? She used to be so smart and everything, but now. She's a mess.*

*I know. Everybody says.*

Everybody says. People talk. Sometimes they talk about things they don't know anything about. Actually, I'm the poster child for people talking about things they don't know anything about.

"Billy, come in," says Granne as the two Greenfields show up at our kitchen door after supper.

I don't wait around. One look at Will's face—unfamiliar and

tense—and I book it down the hall to my room. Granne can think what she wants. Will can think what he wants, too. I can't be here right now.

So, yes, I run away to my room and leave the door open, just enough that I can hear them down the hall in the kitchen. I sit on the edge of my bed, staring at the doorknob, and listen.

"Mrs. D, I have to talk to you," says Billy, and I can hear from his voice that it's out there, the words, the story, the thing everyone is talking about.

And Granne doesn't know yet. She still has her good neighbor, good employer voice going.

"Come in, you two. What's this about?"

So Billy tells her, stuttering a little. I picture him standing just inside the sliding door with Will, his loyal soldier, standing beside him.

"Will here tells me people are talking. About the fire."

"Of course they are, Billy. It's big news in a small town like ours." Granne's still in no-nonsense mode.

"Well, you see, Will here heard some people talking, and they're saying that the fire, it was started—that I started the fire. My smoking started the fire."

A beat, in which I picture Granne standing by the sink where I left her, listening to Billy.

"Were you smoking, Billy? Last night? Were you smoking at the café?"

"Well, yes and no," he says. "You see ... Becca showed up with her rug, and she was asking about hanging it that night, and she asked me to come out to her van and take a look at it, for size and everything. So we could talk about the best way to pin it up there, 'cause it's heavy. So I lit up in the kitchen and took it with me outside to take a look."

"And?" says Granne.

After a moment, he continues. "I was out there for a while. Decided we'd wait to hang it. There was going to be lots of dust and mess with the countertops and appliances, so I said maybe best to wait until that was done, and she thought so, too. And we talked a while and then she left and I went back inside."

"With your cigarette," says Granne.

"Well, that's the thing. I can't remember if I still had it. But I don't think so. I never smoke in there when I'm working.

This sounds so much like a conversation between a student and a teacher, it isn't even funny.

"You know that the firefighters weren't able to determine what started the fire, just where," says Granne. "And that it wasn't electrical. It started along the storage room wall, which is completely burned out, as you know. I thought maybe a soldering iron from one of the plumbers. There's a sink there, and a drain, on the other side of the wall. But ... well, did you even go into the storage room that night, Billy?"

"You see," he pauses again, maybe to swallow. "I did go in there. Just for a minute, just when I came back in from talking to Becca. I closed the window—you know how it sticks—and then I heard my phone out in the kitchen. So if I had a smoke with me ..."

Another silence. I picture Granne, arms folded now, imagining Billy in the storage room with a cigarette, maybe putting it down on the edge of the desk as he goes to close the sticky window that needs two hands, and then he gets distracted by his phone. And is she thinking about that other stuff, too? Like the story about Billy having a drinking problem and burning down the Henwoods' shed ten years ago?

"And what makes you think people are saying you're to blame?"

"Well, Will here came home this morning from the Co-op and said people are saying it was me. Me smoking. And they brought up that old Henwood shed story, and—and all that."

At least, I think that's what he says, because his voice trails off and there's a half-open door and hallway between me and the kitchen.

Which means, if I heard Billy right, Will went to work at the Co-op after about an hour's sleep.

"William, who told you this?"

"Phil, the Scotsburn milk truck driver. He heard it at Henwoods' this morning. And Chelsea's mom. She was on cash today."

He answers quickly and his voice is low and maybe even angry. Angry at his dad for dragging him over here? Or angry at his dad for starting a fire in our café?

Or angry at the Henwoods and Phil the milk truck driver and Chelsea's mom and all the talking people in general?

There's a pause then, and I expect Granne to shoot down the talking people and tell Billy to get back to work and just ignore all this nonsense. But she doesn't.

Granne doesn't say anything and that scares me a little, because if Granne believes, even a little, what people are saying …

"Mrs. D, Dad and I have been talking," says Will, breaking

the silence that is getting way too long and weird. "We're going to finish the repairs on the café and make it perfect. That should shut people up."

I hate the sound of his voice. Harsh. Angry. Not the Will I know at all.

"Of course. Of course," Granne says, but it's as if she's thinking about something else. Why doesn't she tell them it's all okay?

Or tell them they're fired?

"We'll make it right." Unfamiliar Will again.

There's movement then, the door opening.

"We'll be there tomorrow to start the clean-up," says Billy. "Come on, son. Goodnight, Mrs. D."

"Goodnight," says Granne. "Thank you. Thank you for telling me." That's all.

The door slides closed, footsteps thump on the deck and down the stairs, and they're gone.

And from the kitchen, not a sound for a very long time. Then a chair being pulled out.

I have to see. I stand up and open the door, creep down the hall to the kitchen. She's sitting there ramrod straight, just staring out at the shore.

# Lost days

It's Wednesday afternoon, five days since the fire, and I've spent most of my time in my room, escaping into podcasts or music. Or sleeping. Or on a corner of the deck where no one can see me from the road, watching the tide come in, go out. Watching the birds. Picking up the needles and yarn. Putting them down again. Thinking about calling my dad, and then telling myself I shouldn't do that until I get myself together, because the last thing he needs is me losing it on the phone, and him so far away and losing it himself. I text him to say I'm okay but sleeping off the late night at the fire. Tell him Granne's in charge. Tell him all is well. Yeah, right.

In other words, I lose a few days.

Granne's been in town a lot of the time, supervising the clean-up, which is going well, according to what she told me when she returned for supper last night, fish and chips from the highway diner in hand.

She leaves me to my self-imposed cave, and when I sometimes emerge, if she's home, she fills me in on developments. "We got a garbage bin set up, some helpers from the volunteer fire department, and Billy and Will, and people being so kind." I listen but I don't hear.

Because my ears are stopped. Or they're full, maybe. Full of those *people talking*.

It's just that the people I hear talking aren't Phil the milk truck driver and Chelsea's mother. I've fallen back a month (is it only a month?) and I hear Amanda, my best friend since kindergarten, calling me on the phone after that night, telling me what people are saying about me. Asking what really happened before she found me lying on the side of the road as Jonah's car sped off. Thinking she's helping but really just making it worse. And Jonah's voice that night in the car, and his online voice filling my socials with such scary stuff that, when I can't get out of bed, when Dad finds me curled around my phone, making noises that aren't words and aren't exactly crying, either, Dad takes my phone and smashes it. And then he goes to the store and gets me a new phone, with a new number that only he and I know. He takes my computer—"I'm just going to store it away for a while, Lark."

And that other voice, my mother's quavering voice: "Bye now, honey. Love you."

And then Granne again, showing up mid-afternoon to check on me.

"Yes, Granne, I ate an apple. Yes, I drank some water, too."

She's upbeat and no-nonsense. Almost excited: "They got so much done today. We may be able to open sooner than the end of the month now. We'll need those books, though, when you're ready to help with that. I've got Becca enlisted to drive …"

The books. Oh, God. The books again.

She comes home on Wednesday evening after being in town all afternoon, and makes tomato soup and grilled cheese sandwiches that we eat at the kitchen table. I'm actually hungry, and the voices are fading now, and I'm able to ask a few questions about the clean-up. She tells me how hard Will is working, and Billy, too. Shakes her head.

Will.

When we're done, when she says, no, she doesn't need any help cleaning up the kitchen, I take the quilt from the mud room and walk down to the shore. Sit there watching the waves break over the sandbars and think about drifting off to Prince Edward

Island. Or Seafoam, maybe. Think about kayaking with Will and watching those seals launch themselves off the sinking reef into the rising tide.

I wait. I wait until the sun is down and the stars are out. I just wait, letting the water and air chase everything else out of my ears, out of my head. I wait and try not to keep looking over my shoulder, listening for the sound of footsteps coming over the point. Listening for anything.

Nothing. Nothing but water and air.

So, after what feels like a few hours, I stand up, shake out the sandy quilt, bundle it under my arm, and pick my way in the dark along the shore back to Granne's house, alone.

# Coffee run

Granne unloads her brilliant idea at about three o'clock on Thursday afternoon.

"Larkin, William, we need a coffee and tea run and you two need a break, so off you go to the bakery. Here's a twenty to cover it. Get whatever you like, but be sure to bring some back for us. Especially the coffee, right, Billy? Cream and sugar in both."

She and I are working at a card table she brought in to use as a desk. She's on her spreadsheets again, also taking advantage of the post-fire-restored Wi-Fi to email suppliers about rescheduling deliveries of tables and chairs and all that stuff. I've been assigned the job of going through a stack of local newspapers, church bulletins, library newsletters, and random flyers to see where we might be able to find or advertise for book donations. This would be so much easier to do online, but clearly she and Dad have had a conversation about this and no computer is provided for me.

She holds the twenty-dollar bill across the table at me, giving it a shake as if to make it fly into my hands.

I really don't want to take it, because that means being forced to walk out the door with Will, sit in the truck beside him, go inside, and stand in line at the bakery. I might even have to talk to him for the next twenty minutes or so. Or maybe not—the talking part, I mean. Will hasn't looked my way or spoken to me since the night of the fire, when he offered to drive me home.

"Uh, Granne, I'm not really hungry," I say without looking over at Will. He's in the kitchen area, laying flooring with his dad.

"Yeah, Mrs. D, we're nearly done here, I don't think—" he says.

We're on the same page, obviously. I guess that's something.

"Nonsense. If I have to make it an order, I will. The two of you—go, now." She smacks the bill on the table and looks annoyed, eyes on her computer screen.

The principal has spoken.

"Go on, Willie, I need my coffee," says Billy from somewhere under the framework of the as-yet uninstalled kitchen counter. "Go."

"Okay, okay." He stands up—*Willie*, that is—and brushes off the knees of his jeans, digs the truck keys out of his jacket hanging on the stepladder, and heads for the door, giving me a "let's go" head tilt on the way.

The bakery is just on the other side of town, and it takes us less than five minutes to get there. Five very quiet minutes, because neither of us talks the whole way.

Then, once we're parked, as I'm about to reach for the door handle, he says: "He didn't do it, you know."

Ah. Finally. I let out a sigh, maybe a sigh of relief, as if I just heard him come over the point in the dark.

I turn my head to look at him, just quickly, because looking people square in the face is not something I'm great at right now.

"I know."

He's been looking straight ahead at the bakery, but now he turns, squints at me.

"You do? Pretty sure Mrs. D doesn't."

I completely agree with him but I don't say that out loud.

He turns back to the big sign above the bakery windows— *Brenda's Bakery, Fresh Daily, Just Like Home*—but I'm pretty sure he's not seeing it. I expect he's back in our kitchen that night with his father, fighting back against all the people talking.

How to explain to him that I understand the need to prove

people wrong, using whatever words or tools you have handy? And when you have no words or tools, when you're completely helpless and empty and lost, you let your dad smash your phone and send you away for the summer.

"I think—I think you're right, what you're doing. Showing people, you know? Showing them they're wrong and you're not going to run away and hide."

I should stop talking, because I'm not sure now if I'm talking about his dad and him, or talking about my dad and me. Dad and me and what we should be doing.

"You do?"

"Yeah, I do."

He shakes his head, still looking out at something that isn't there. "It's such a small town. Everybody knows everything." Yup. He's speaking my language now. "I can't wait to get out of here," he says then. "One more year, then university. That's if I can survive one more year of the jerks at my high school. And if I can afford it."

"I think probably every high school is full of jerks," I say, and think about adding, *speaking from experience,* but don't, because then I might have to explain.

"Tuttle Harbour takes the prize, though."

It's short and sharp, like the voice I heard from him in the kitchen that night.

Now it's my turn to stare out the front windshield at nothing. No, not at nothing—at the long crowded hallway on the day I came in to write the first of my final exams in the Accommodations room. Walking down the hall beside Mrs. Varma and pretending I'm invisible and no one is looking at me. Me and my periorbital hematoma.

I sense Will's looking at me now, though. Looking at me and maybe getting ready to ask about the jerks in my world.

So I shrug, say, "Let's get the stuff," and wave the twenty in the air. "Maybe a coffee and a giant ginger-molasses cookie will fix everything."

He actually laughs at that. "Yeah, Brenda's cookies are like magic."

*I made him laugh.*

That's what I'm thinking as I climb out of the truck and lead the way up the steps into the bakery. He opens the door for me and we go inside, like any other teenagers on coffee break from their summer jobs.

Chelsea's there behind the counter. How did I forget that she works here? She smiles hugely and waves, "Hey guys!" so I smile back, because I just rode in a vehicle with a boy who doesn't scare me. And I made him laugh.

# Report card

"Hi, Dad."

"Hey, Lark. Great to hear your voice, honey."

I know he means this because I've been shutting down his texted requests for a call. I don't know if he wants to talk about my stuff or his stuff with Mom, but I know I haven't been ready to talk about anybody's stuff for a few days.

But now it's Thursday, and I survived a day on the job and a trip to the bakery in a truck with Will, so I've got this because, after all, Brenda's cookies ... right? I ate a whole enormous soft chocolate chip by myself, and part of Granne's ginger-molasses-spice so yeah, I'm feeling the magic.

"You've been busy?" he asks, giving me an out. I'm pretty sure he knows I've been oh-so-busy hiding out in my room or on a corner of the deck, trying to get the smell of smoke and the sound of people talking out of my head.

"Yeah, we've been busy getting the café cleaned up and everything."

"How's it going?"

"Good. Good. Listen, Dad, my marks came and I thought you'd want to know I passed Grade 10."

"I had an idea that was a sure thing." I can hear him smiling. "Lynette forwarded your mail, then? Good." Most people check their marks online, of course, but no computer and limited data on my phone, not to mention strict instructions from Dad to stay off any browsers. Easy instruction, actually.

"Yeah, it came today. So, I guess that means Grade 11." And I stop there because it's something we haven't really talked about yet. Grade 11. Going back to school in the fall. With all those people.

"Look, Lark," he sighs. "Can we just park that conversation for a while? You know, lots going on with both of us, and that's something we can talk about in person when I get there."

"Do you know when you're coming?"

He sighs again. "No, no, not yet. Soon, though, I promise. Some stuff is happening here—can't fill you in yet, but I will soon, I promise."

Okay, I know it's not a great thing when someone doesn't

want to tell you what's going on, and especially when that someone is your father and he's talking about your mother in rehab. A little hum starts growing somewhere in my head and I try hard to shut it down by asking about other stuff, like what he's doing right now.

"Sitting in Starbucks, me and Jimmy Perez," he says right away, and I can hear the smile back in his voice. "Good coffee and a good mystery."

"Alone?" I ask it cautiously, in case my grandparents are sitting there eavesdropping.

"Yup. That's the best part," he laughs. "The only thing that would make it better is if you were here, too."

And immediately, the good feels evaporate and the hum gets louder. He tries to rescue the moment.

"What about you? Where are you right now?" Making an effort to sound all hearty and upbeat.

"Just in my room. I might go for a walk on the beach soon, though. Watch the sunset."

"Great. The best sunsets happen on that beach, and I'm speaking from experience."

Okay, the hum fades and it sounds normal again.

"Back to work at the café tomorrow?"

"Actually, no. I'm going on a road trip."

"Interesting. You and Granne?"

"Nope. Me and Becca. We're going to pick up some book donations from some churches and places along the shore."

"Becca, eh? Sounds like fun." Hmmm. I avoid asking why hanging out with Becca sounds like fun, in case he launches into some personal anecdote. "And listen to you. 'Along the shore.' You sound like a local."

"Ha … yeah. That's me."

"Becca Patriquin. You could do a lot worse than go road-tripping with Becca. Tell her I say hi and I'll catch up with her when I'm down. Is her son there, too?"

Son? What son? Becca has a son?

But I play it cool. "No, don't think so. Haven't seen him, anyway."

Pretty sure there was no sign of a son—or a husband or anyone else—that day I dropped in. That day or ever.

"Well, that'll be fun. Driving *along the shore*," he puts on his best local accent and sounds just like Billy Greenfield. And then he lowers his voice. "Oops. Some couple at the next table just looked at me funny. Geez, these West Coast cool kids just don't appreciate a good East Coast accent when they hear it."

We sign off shortly after that, both of us sending love and hugs. Both of us sounding like we've got our acts together.

So it's a good thing I didn't tell him about the other piece of mail that came in the envelope Lynette sent. A letter from Amanda.

*Your friend dropped by to find out your address, so I said I would just send it along with your report. Hope you're having a good time. Lynette.* She wrote it on Amanda's sealed envelope.

Her letter is printed off from the computer and full of news of summer back in the neighborhood. Some of it news that Dad doesn't need to hear right now.

*Hey Lark,*

*I MISS you!! Xoxoxoxo When are you coming home? Or are you staying with your grandmother for the whole summer? It's so boring here without you. The job at the day camp is okay, but some of the kids are so annoying and whiney. And some are very sweet so I guess it evens out. But you were supposed to be here with me and that would have been so much fun!!!! There's a couple of really cute guys on staff named Matt and Arvo (I know, eh?) and they're from*

St. Matthew's, the Catholic high school, so that makes it INTERESTING if you know what I MEAN. One of the other counselors is a girl named Ambre from Northwood Heights and we've been hanging out together. She has a pool so we go after work and cool off. She asked Matt and Arvo so they might be coming over on Saturday, too. It's not nearly as fun as hanging out with you, of course!!!

I hope you're having a nice time out there with your grandmother. Is that even possible??? I don't know her. Maybe she's more fun than my grandmother. She watches TV all day and drinks a whole bottle of wine at night. (I've met Amanda's grandmother and this is an exaggeration. Amanda does exaggerate, but she's funny when she does it, most of the time.) I hope you're hanging out at the beach and having a great time.

Hey, I know it was a crap way to end the year. I wish I could change everything. If you want to know anything about anybody back here, just write me a letter. Or if your dad says it's okay, send me a text from your new number. Or email. I'm not emailing you anything cause I know your dad has your computer and that would be quite AWKWARD. But write me. PLEASE WRITE ME so I know you're okay and all that shit from the party etc etc is just over and done with. Jonah's still cruising around as if nothing happened, *but people are still talking, of course. He actually asked me where you were this summer, if you can believe it. He is SUCH a dick and maybe more people know that now. I HOPE SO! But you know what it's like. Jasmine and I haven't been talking much because she's all about Sam, that friend of Jonah's, and hanging out with those people. Maybe I should warn her? I tell everyone you're doing great out there and I'm sure you are. Right? RIGHT? I've got your back, whatever happens. Next year will be better. Hey, did you get your grades? I passed! Nearly failed History, though. Maybe because you weren't beside me during the exam! So just ignore everyone and come back and be my best friend again because it's just not the same here without you. LOVE YOU!!! HUGS!!! Xoxoxo Mandy*

Yeah. Full of news I don't really want to hear, either.

# Road trip with Becca

"Take them, Becca. I mean it. Take the lot," says the lady in the United Church hall somewhere near Malagash, waving her arm at the boxes and bags of books stacked around the walls of the cloak room. "I was just sick when I heard about that fire. Poor Anne!"

It's been like this pretty much all day at every stop along the winding road.

Becca and I get out of her car at a church hall or house or general store or Women's Institute building (*W.I.N.S. FOR HOME AND COUNTRY*). I stand by as Becca launches into a few minutes of friendly conversation with whatever person comes to meet us— "And you're Anne's granddaughter," they say as they give me the big welcome treatment—mostly women but there was also one old guy cutting grass. They ask about Becca's business, which I finally figure out is the making and selling of hooked rugs, along with teaching people how to do it. She's an artist—"Your show in Halifax, can't wait to get down there" and "Send us the info on your September courses and we'll spread the word." Lots of chat about sheep, and wool, and her website. And then, finally, the conversation turns to the used books, always with the words: "For Anne."

I had no idea my grandmother and her Tuttle Harbour Café and Reading Room project were so well known.

I also had no idea there were so many people with books they wanted to give away. We already had a lot of books—now turned into ashes, of course—but they just seem to keep coming. This is our last stop and Becca's suv is jammed.

"Aw, Aggie, this is great," she says to the Malagash lady, as I start my job of lugging the donations to the van, where I play Tetris with the boxes and bags in the back. The storage space is getting full. "We can't believe how generous people are."

"Well, it was such a setback for her. You know we're all behind her," says Aggie, who looks about Granne's age. Maybe a teaching buddy. "When I heard about that fire, I was just sick for her. Do they know how it started?"

Ah. The big question that keeps popping up. Becca has been careful to sidestep this one. "Just one of those things." "Nope, but the clean-up is going great." "They caught it quickly and the room full of book donations was really the only casualty." Etc. Etc.

And we say thanks and drive away.

"I don't believe for a minute that Billy started that fire," she says to me at the start of the trip, shortly after we leave Tuttle Harbour Friday morning with our tea and a giant molasses-ginger cookie to share.

Clearly Becca wants to set the tone. Getting it all out there. No gossip or "people are saying" tolerated here. And that's just fine with me.

I'm still hugging that conversation with Will to myself, like a little gold medal in acting normal. "Me, neither."

So now me and Becca, we're teammates.

She leaves it there and moves on to the plan for the day, mostly names of places—Tatamagouche, Malagash, Marshville, Brule Point, River John, Heathbell, Scotsburn—that mean nothing to me. We start at the furthest point, so the initial drive is uninterrupted by stops, and we talk.

I had been worried about this part. I mean, what would we talk *about*? I like her and everything, and I don't feel nervous or whatever around her, but you never know what to expect, when you're stuck in a vehicle with someone you don't know well for hours at a time. I mean, what if she asks about home? About school? My friends? All the usual stuff that most kids my age talk about?

Or even worse, my parents. My mom. My dad …

But she doesn't. Right after we get our tea and cookies ("Break it in two, Larkin. Take the biggest part for yourself." And I do it, because these cookies are *magic*), she says something introductory about the two of us driving off to work, and how it will be a nice way for me to see some of the countryside. And also how it should be easy because people have been in touch already with offers of help, which is what happens when you're as well respected and well liked as Anne is.

And that's when she pauses, looks over at me, and says the thing about Billy and the fire.

And after that, we just talk, listening to some oldies station, maybe the same one Will plays in the truck. We talk about other stuff, too.

"Have you had a chance to join the kids at the back shore? At Henwoods' little beach and fire pit? That's always been a hot spot during the summer."

"Yeah." How much to say? How much does she know? Is this a fishing question? You never know with adults. "The first week I was here, I went over there. With Will."

"Oh, nice. Will's such a sweetie, isn't he?"

No comment. Dangerous territory, and I know better than to agree with her and start the conversation about what a great guy Will is. Or what happened the night Will and I went over to the fire pit at the Henwoods' beach on the back shore.

My tea is still good and hot between my hands. The magic cookie has performed its spell—I've unclenched my jaw and the muscles around my neck and shoulders, all without having to remind myself to count and breathe. The view ahead is of long stretches of two-lane country road, rising and falling through fields and forests and occasional marshes full of tall grass, with the Northumberland Strait, hyper-blue against the summer green, off to our left, close then far. Gone—then we come over a hill and there it is again. As if it's moving along with us.

"I never get tired of this drive," says Becca at one point, after passing through a couple of towns and pushing back out into the green fields. In the distance, a height, like a mountain.

"We're not going that far, but you can see Wentworth over

there." She points toward the height of land looking a bit hazy in the growing heat of the day. "I used to go skiing there with my son."

Okay. The son. I wonder if it's safe to ask about him. I mean, this son must have had a father, and there's been no mention or sign of any man in her life. Still, I'm curious.

"You have a son?"

"I do." She smiles that proud mom smile I've seen on other moms. "Sean. He's a student at Dalhousie, but this summer he's doing a co-op placement at Memorial in St. John's. Newfoundland, you know?" She turns to make sure I'm up to speed on Canadian universities and geography. "He's consumed with the science of ocean ice, pack ice, all that stuff, and they have a program over there that he wants to get into for grad school."

University and grad school means he's older. I'm still wondering about Sean's dad, though.

"Is he enjoying it?"

"Very much. And there's a bonus." She throws a quick grin my way. "They have a lot of pubs in St. John's. A lot of pubs and music and musicians, and Sean's a great guitarist and a not-bad singer, so he's having lots of fun down on George Street, too."

A musician. The artistic gene, clearly.

"Remember I told you about that band your dad was in? With Billy and those very cool brothers from Linden? Well, I actually ended up marrying one of those very cool brothers. Sean's dad." She says this while keeping her eyes on the road, which I know means something is coming. Divorce?

"He passed away from cancer about seventeen years ago, when Sean was barely in school."

Ah. "I'm so sorry."

"Thank you. Yes, it was very hard at the time, but it's funny how you just kind of do what you have to do to survive something tough like that." She sounds calm about it all, but I guess that's what happens when you've had seventeen years to deal with a bad thing.

Quick arithmetic: in seventeen years I'll be thirty-three.

"So it was just Sean and me for a while." I'm getting the life story but I actually don't mind. "And then my parents started to go downhill. First my dad with dementia, then my mom with a whole bunch of illnesses, so I gave up my teaching job in Halifax and we moved back here to the Point. Dad's been gone for five years now and Mom died about three years ago, when Sean was off at Dal, and I just stayed. Doing some supply teaching at the high school.

Making my rugs. Spreading a little art around when I can."

When I glance at her, she's smiling. Remembering these things, even sad things, makes her smile.

"How's the knitting going?"

"Great. Good. I've used up one skein and I'm partway through the other," I say.

"Isn't that the most gorgeous yarn?" She shakes her head in fiber awe. "My friend Marnie, over near Wallace, spins and hand-dyes it from her own sheep. It feels like I'm working with pure gold when I use it on my rugs."

"Yeah, I like the feel of it under my fingers. It's so, so soft. So smooth. It just slides on and off the needles." Listen to me, all artsy. But it's true. The brilliant blue-green yarn is textured and smooth and silky. Just holding the needles and guiding the yarn around them to make stitches is so soothing, so quiet, like an invisible voice in my head, saying, "Shhh. Good. Shhh." I don't say that, though, because that would just sound weird.

"I know … right?" Becca laughs. "There is nothing like working with the best fiber. You can even make mistakes and it still looks fabulous."

"It'll be a nice scarf when I'm done. I'm thinking of giving it to my dad."

"Perfect," says Becca.

We're quiet then for a while and the first town, Scotsburn, is in sight, so I realize that sharing time is over, which is too bad.

Because it occurs to me that someone like Becca, someone who watched her husband and her parents die and raised a kid by herself, and is a successful artist and has her life together, and is easy to talk to and is not related to me—someone like that could probably give someone like me tips on finding my way back to normal.

# What is normal?

I'm sitting on the shore, again. Watching the sunset and the waves rolling over the sandbars, again. Thinking about swimming to Prince Edward Island, again.

Wondering if Will is going to come over the point and sit beside me, run his fingers through the sand the way he does, and talk with me, again.

So far, no. Again.

I'm thinking about Becca and our trip today, the easy conversation, the sense of … I don't know … *comfort* that surrounds her. Becca, who is not my mother or anyone close to me, but who I think might be someone I could talk to.

Talk about being normal.

Because, after all, do I even know what normal looks like anymore?

I did, once upon a time. Once upon a time, before the car

accident, it looked like a mommy and a daddy and a little girl who likes drawing at the kitchen table, while Mom makes supper after her day working at the university library. And bike rides to the park together on weekends. And after-dinner walks with Dad to look for bugs. And reading together at bedtime. Yes, that's what my normal looked like.

Then, after that guy ran a red light and Mom and I were tossed around inside the car, normal changed. Normal becomes Mom lying on the couch, watching TV, and me drawing at the kitchen table, but looking up because she's wiping her eyes as if she's crying. "I'm fine, Larkin. Mommy's back is hurting today, but I'm just going to take my medicine and I'll be fine."

Normal becomes Dad taking me to Story Time at the library because Mom is locked in the bathroom and she says she's sick, we should go without her. Normal becomes Dad organizing my eighth birthday party because Mom isn't home.

"But where is she, Dad?

"She's just out, Lark. She's busy. It's okay, I'm an expert at party planning—it's going to be great."

Normal becomes whispered arguments that they think I can't hear, then loud arguments that I can hear just fine.

"You don't know what it's like, Andy."

"But Charlotte, you've got to get this under control. It's affecting Larkin."

And my mother crying. "I'm trying, Andy. Why don't you believe me?"

And then, later, "Leave me alone, for fuck's sake. Can't you see how much pain I'm in? I'm trying, Andy, just fucking leave me alone."

And my dad, asking what he can do to help, pleading with her to see a doctor. "I'll take you. We'll do this together."

I'm in my room huddled against the door so I can hear, arms wrapped around my stuffy, Hedwig, a large owl. "Just shut up, Andy. I'm going out."

My dad's pleading voice but I can't make out the words. Slamming doors. Silence for a long time, then sounds from the kitchen. And when Hedwig and I finally open my bedroom door and creep down the hall toward the kitchen, my dad is there making supper. He looks over his shoulder at me and smiles and I feel better. "Hungry, Lark? Supper coming right up."

And normal changes again when Mom goes to Vancouver to visit my grandparents for a week. The week turns into a month.

Into two months. Six months. Normal is breakfast with Dad, walking to school with Amanda and her little brother, lunch at Amanda's house, back to Amanda's after school, sometimes sleeping over at Amanda's, her mother hugging me and tucking me in just like Amanda, and me forgetting what my mom used to say at bedtime. Was it "Night, night, sleep tight?" Or was it "Now I lay me down to sleep?" Normal is home from Amanda's with Dad, and doing homework at the kitchen table while he marks essays or works on his computer.

"Larkin, Mom's going to stay in Vancouver a while longer. She sick and she's trying to get better."

Normal is not talking about Mom.

And then middle school, which is fun and busy and exciting, at first. Trying out for teams, and running for student council. Being in charge of the book fair. But then a panicky call from Vancouver and Dad has to leave me at Amanda's house while he flies out there to figure it out. And when he gets back, he's different—sad and worried—even though he tries to hide it from me. And so then the books thing, and the crying in class starts. Always the parent-teacher interviews with just Dad. It's just normal.

"Larkin, Mom's in a special hospital. She's going to stay in Vancouver a while longer."

The awkward summer visits with Grandma Sylvia and Grandpa John. Visits with my mother sitting on a bench in the hospital garden, trying to smile and talk to me, but looking as if she's a puppet and some unseen hand is moving her lips. My stick-figure mother falling asleep while I try to think of something to say to her, and Dad taking me by the hand and walking us away when the nurse comes.

And finally, high school. So many new people. Even the kids I've known forever seem unfamiliar now. The boys, especially. Amanda and her crush on that guy Tim, and convincing me to go to the school dance with her and Tim and Tim's friend, Dev. That's normal, right? Going to a school dance? But when Dev leans close to me and says, "Wanna dance?" I feel as if something is choking me. I can't breathe, and I tell him I don't feel well and have to call my dad. I back away from him and Dev shrugs and doesn't follow me, as I tell the teachers at the door that my dad is coming to pick me up because I'm sick.

"Is everything all right, Larkin?"

"Yes, fine, I just don't feel well all of a sudden."

And the look, the teacher look, the adult look. "Did something happen to upset you, Larkin?"

"No, nothing, everything's fine." *Where are you, Dad? Get me out of here, please …*

And then another kind of normal, discovered at Amanda's when her parents are out and she shows me their booze stash, and how good it feels to just drink all that feeling away. Now my normal is to feel everything, drink something, and feel nothing until the next day. And hope Dad doesn't notice, which is easy because he's distracted now.

Lynette becomes part of the normal, too.

"My friend Lynette's coming over for supper tonight, Lark—is that okay?" And "Lynette's going to join us for Christmas dinner. She's on her own." And "Lynette's apartment is being renovated, so she's going to stay with us for a while—I hope you're okay with that, Lark."

I don't care. It helps, really, because with Lynette there, my dad doesn't see me as closely anymore. She isn't my mother, so I can ignore her and not feel guilty. Not feel guilty about ignoring her, anyway.

Normal is the guilt. Normal is feeling, followed by not

feeling. Normal is the next day, and there I am with my head in the toilet. The guilt again. The fear. *I'm just like my mother.* That's my normal.

"Larkin, Mom's going to stay in Vancouver a while longer."

And then going to the end-of-classes party a month ago with Amanda.

And Jonah is there—beautiful Jonah, who all the girls talk about, all the girls want. But at this party, as it gets late and a bit hazy, he seems to want me. "C'mon, Larkin, I've been wanting to talk to you for so long. I've got some good stuff in my car."

Why not? This great-looking guy wants me. That's normal, right? Right?

So now I'm here at Granne's with my bruises and my guilt and my fear of pretty much everything, and I know I know I know this can't be normal.

# Eavesdropping

"Suzanne, how nice to see you," says Granne, out in the main room of the café.

No idea who Suzanne is, so I just keep working in the recently transformed storage room, which now has shelves and a little table and new walls and floor and ceiling. That's what burning down part of a building will do. In the hands of a good builder like Billy, it turns into a brightly lit, white-walled hideout for me and my book donations.

They're stacked in boxes and piled up in bags against one wall, under the table, and on some of the shelves. With the little window open, it's actually kind of cozy. I'm doing okay. No one can see me unless they lean around the half-closed door and look in—and mostly nobody looks in.

Everything is still under construction but nearly done, especially in the kitchen, where Billy and Will have finished the flooring, the cabinets, and the counters. The electrician was here. The plumber was here. Now Billy has started painting the kitchen walls, and Will came in this afternoon after his shift at the Co-op to help. It's nearly done and it looks amazing.

"Wow, you're nearly done," says Suzanne, whoever she is. "It looks great, Anne. When does the furniture come?"

"Tables and chairs tomorrow," says Granne. "Kitchen appliances on Thursday and Friday. Inspections early next week and we hope to open the door—quietly open the door, mind you—by the end of next week."

It's nice that she says "*we* hope"—recognizing the team effort.

Some team, though. Billy is in silent get-it-done mode. Will is, too. Granne is just Granne. Going non-stop, as usual.

And I'm just keeping my head down. I sort the books into piles and repack them, creating an inventory list on an Excel spreadsheet. Yes, on a computer. No, I don't know the Wi-Fi password, so I'm not tempted to check mail or open a browser.

"Your father said no computer time," she says when she hands me her old Toshiba laptop the day after Becca and I do our roundup along the shore. "But I don't think that includes record keeping, do you?"

"No, I'm pretty sure record keeping is okay."

"You know Excel?"

"Yup."

She hands it over. Pauses.

"The Wi-Fi is turned off on this computer for now—you understand that, Larkin."

Okay, that's just a little humiliating, but I get it. Nod without looking at her. "Right. Good."

It is good, actually. Being disconnected from Amanda and social media and people talking back home is a good place to be. And look at me: handling books, reading a little bit here and there, typing titles and authors and publishers into the tiny columns and cells, and putting things in order. Me. Putting things in order in a room full of books. Mrs. Varma and every Language Arts teacher from my past would be astounded.

"Hey, Mom."

I look up from the Louise Penny hardcover I just flipped open and watch the half-closed doorway. Suzanne is Will's mom?

"Hey, bud. It's looking great in here."

"Thanks. Yeah, it's mostly Dad."

"Looking so great, Bill," says this Suzanne person, sounding all happy and bright. Maybe she's heard people talking. Maybe she sees that Billy has been working like a robot, expressionless and mostly silent and, I don't know, driven. Maybe she's trying to cheer him up.

"Yup, we're getting it done." Billy sounds as if he might be smiling, maybe looking over his shoulder while still painting.

"It will be so exciting when you open, Anne. Any big plans? You'll have to have an official opening at some point." Suzanne avoids any mention of delays due to her husband (word on the street) burning half the café down a few weeks ago.

"I agree, but not right away," Granne says. "And how are you doing, Suzanne? Still at the Lodge?"

There's a brief conversation then about Suzanne's job at the Lodge (whatever that is), how busy she is, how the dear old things make her smile, though. The Lodge—a place for old people, maybe?

"There but for the grace of God," says Granne, but she sounds pretty unreligious as she says it. Hard to imagine Granne in an old people's home. "Do you need your men, Suzanne? They can wrap it up here now if you need them."

"No, no problem. But, Will, this came for you today."

It's quiet out there. I hear Will thunk down his paint roller in the tray, and then there's a movement at my partly open door as he passes on his way to the front room. I'm dying to follow him, to check out his mother, to see what came for him in the mail. Yes, dying to follow him, but I don't want to look as if I'm following him, so I stay standing at the table, Louise Penny still in my hands.

An envelope being opened maybe, and then the rattle of paper. Then Will.

"I got it." I can tell from his voice that he's smiling.

"Oh, Will, that's just wonderful," says Suzanne. "The county science award, Anne. The one you wrote that reference letter for."

"Congratulations, William! I couldn't be happier." Granne sounds pretty happy, all right.

"Good for you, son." Billy says from the kitchen, and he might be smiling, too, but it's hard to tell.

"They say I can use it for that special program week at Dal during March Break ... or save it for university tuition ... whatever."

"I knew you'd get it." Proud mom.

"How could he not?" Granne says. "What do you think, William? That March Break program at Dalhousie is excellent.

Remember Taylor Arsenault? She did it a few years ago and she's there now, getting ready for medical school. I could give you her email if you want to ask her about it."

"Oh, yeah … okay … thanks, Mrs. D," Will says. "I think maybe for now I'll just put it in the bank. You know, until I figure out what I'm doing."

"Good idea," says Granne.

I put Louise Penny down and inch toward the door because I want to get a glimpse of Will's mom and see what's happening out there, but how do I walk out in the middle of this conversation?

"Good idea," says Billy. But he doesn't stop. I can still hear him rolling paint onto the kitchen wall.

"Here, Mom. Can you take it home? Just put it on my desk."

"Of course. Give it to me. And when will you two be home?"

"Dad?"

"You can head off any time, Will. Any time. I'm just going to stay here and get this wall done. And put the drawers back in, and change those drawer pulls."

"Billy," says Granne. It's a voice I've never heard. Not her teacher voice—well, yes, a teacher voice. Like when that nice, hardworking kid who always fails math tests just failed another math test. "That can all wait. You and Will clean up and go home. It's been a long day and you must be tired."

The only sound is the roller pressing out its paint on the rebuilt kitchen walls.

I think he grunts, then, "I'll just finish this wall."

Will passes the door again, I'm guessing to go clean up his painting tools. If he looked in the partly open door, he'd see me standing there frozen halfway between the table and the doorway like the eavesdropper I am. But he doesn't look.

"Anne, is Larkin here? I'd love to meet her."

Saved!

"Larkin?" Granne calls me, so I pick up Louise Penny and replace her noisily on the table, give the table a little shove as if I'm squeezing by it. Yup, that's me. Just hanging out here in the storage room, not listening to a word anyone's saying out there in the café.

"Yes, here."

Will's mother is round, fair-haired. He looks a lot like her, actually. She's wearing a loose pink V-necked top and matching pants, nurse clothes, and, as I come around the corner from the storage room, she comes forward, smiling at me with her hand out.

"Oh, Larkin, you're so like your dad. Lovely to meet you, dear," she says, shaking my hand without actually shaking it. Sort of holding it, giving it a little squeeze, and then letting go.

Great. Suzanne's another one of the cool kids from high school who knows my dad.

"Hi."

"Will says you had a nice time out on the kayaks the other night. I'm sorry I missed you, but I work shifts and I'm sometimes not around in the evenings." Mrs. Greenfield tilts her head to one side when she talks, and I recognize Will in that action. As if they're making sure they're not coming on too strong.

"It was great, but I'm not very good at it," I say, making polite conversation. "The seals were pretty neat, though."

And there's some chat about the seals, and the herons, and the beach, and swimming when the jellyfish infest the water in late June and early July. She asks about Dad and not Mom, and I tell her he's coming soon. I don't know how much she knows, but she doesn't let me see anything other than her smiling face.

And then Will's beside me and she looks up at him and I can see how much she adores him.

"Come on, Willie boy, let's get going and maybe your dad will get the hint."

Everyone laughs, chuckles, smiles at her little joke.

"So lovely to meet you at last, Larkin," she says just before going through the door.

"Thank you … you, too."

"See you, Anne. It looks fantastic."

"Great to see you, too, Suzanne. Come over for an evening visit some time when you're on days and have the energy. Love to catch up with you," says Granne.

Waves, smiles—and they're gone. Will follows his mom down the steps off the café porch and they're talking, laughing together. I watch them through the screen door and, just as I'm about to turn back to Louise Penny and friends in the storage room, I see Will stop, say something to his mom and turn back. He jogs across the porch and opens the door. Looks at me, still standing there beside Granne.

"Hey, tide'll be coming in tonight. Interested in kayaking after supper?"

"Sure." I nod without even thinking about it.

"Great. I'll have everything ready. Just come on over whenever."

"Okay."

The door snaps shut and he jumps off the porch to catch up to his mom.

Granne leans across the card table and closes her laptop.

"That's our cue, Billy. Time to go."

"All right, then, Mrs. D. I hear you," he says, gives me that shy sideways smile of his, and finally puts his paint roller down. "Can't argue with the rising tide, can we?"

# On the water

The clouds have rolled in. I watch this huge gray mass creep across the sky from the southwest and turn the water of the Northumberland Strait a sort of silvery purple color, as we leave town and turn onto the road toward Granne's house.

Rain. Shit. I really, really want to go kayaking with Will.

It doesn't rain, though. The wind drops and these clouds just turn the air heavy and still, like they're throwing a blanket over everything.

Granne glances out the kitchen window as we clear the table after supper. "Go on, now. Get your kayaking in before the wind comes up."

"Okay."

"Life jackets, Larkin. Don't forget."

"Yeah, Will has them. See you later, Granne."

She turns from the sink to see me go and, just for a moment,

I see a faint resemblance to my dad—that tired smile and eyes slightly squinty, as if she's thinking something she's not going to say out loud. Dad does exactly the same thing. Words unspoken are something I hear all the time.

But then she smiles. This time a real smile. "Have fun."

He's waiting for me when I come over the point. The kayaks are sitting on the red sand, half in the water, double-bladed paddles already on board.

"Here." He hands me the bright yellow life jacket. "I'm sure you got the lecture, right?"

That makes me laugh. "You, too?"

"Oh, yeah. And sometimes I get the story about Algie Bonnan, the lobster fisherman, who drowned in the harbor when he fell out of his boat. No life jacket. Couldn't swim." He shrugs. "Life around the water, I guess. Parents, eh?"

"Yeah." Well, in my case, a guardian grandmother.

We're on the water now, the perfectly calm and glassy rising tide. No whisper of wind, no ripples, except from our kayaks and paddles. We set off from Will's beach and head along the shore, around the point, and out toward the reef, which is already almost under water. A few tall black sea birds stand there, watching us approach, but they take off, skimming across the water, before we get close.

"Cormorants," Will says. "Seals must all be under already."

And like that, a sleek gray head pops up out of the water in front of us. Two huge black eyes, a doggy snout, whiskers. We stop paddling—me in surprise—and the seal looks at us, then heads out to open water and disappears. All without a sound.

"That was so cool." I know he's probably thinking I sound like the city kid I am, but I just can't help myself. That wild animal face so close—it's like I'm living in a giant zoo.

"I know, eh? Let's go ahead a bit and then, take a really slow look over your shoulder."

"Why?"

"You'll see."

So we do. We paddle for about a minute and then stop, and when I turn carefully to look behind me, there are six pairs of round black eyes on six sleek silver heads sticking up out of the water, watching us. Following. Not creepy or stalky or anything. It's more like being followed by a pack of puppies.

"Wow." I look over at him and my face must say it all.

"Yeah, I know."

The air is soft. Soft and heavy at the same time, maybe because the clouds are so low. And it's quiet. Our paddles dip and splash—well, mostly only my paddles splash—as we follow the shore. We go pretty far, past the deserted Henwood beach— "Maybe they're haying, trying to get it in before it rains," says Will—along a shoreline of big red boulders and sand and sea grass, with low red shorelines rising to mini-cliffs topped by scrubby pines. We pass three points of land past Henwoods', past two coves full of mostly rocks and seaweed.

Sometimes I just stop paddling and drift so I can hear how quiet it is. At our furthest point, I hear voices carried over the water from small white houses up ahead along the shore.

"Summer people." Will nods at them. "They're the loudest."

He's right—they are loud, especially in this windless, blue-gray world of water and sky. And us, with our paddles splitting the surface and the swish of our kayaks leaving a trail of ripples in the water behind us. We drift some more and eventually the voices stop. Maybe they've gone inside—after all, the light is fading from the sky now. It's getting later.

We should probably be getting back, but not yet.

"I love how quiet it is out here," I say.

I look out across the Northumberland Strait, where the water and sky have merged, and I can't tell where one stops and the other starts. Somewhere over there, suspended in between water and sky, is Prince Edward Island. Will drifts into my line of vision and he's leaning back, eyes closed.

"Yeah, me, too. Nobody talking."

Nobody talking sounds like heaven to me right now. In fact, I think maybe this is the best place I've been, the best moment I've lived, for days. Maybe weeks.

Actually, this moment right here on the water with Will might be the best moment I've lived for years.

"Hey, we should turn around," he says, but he doesn't start paddling. I don't, either.

We just drift together for a few more minutes.

"Come on," he says then, and he sticks out his paddle and gives my kayak a tap. "Time to go. My mom made scones, and she said you have to come in when we get back or her feelings will be hurt."

I need to capture this moment, store it somewhere so that I can pull it out when I need it—the water and sky, the muted far-off evening sounds, and the silence right here around me. The seals. This boy.

It's getting dark now but we can see people at Henwoods' beach as we paddle by. We're too far out to see who it is or whose voices we can hear. They're lighting the fire, too, and I can see Casey's fancy ATV parked in the lane behind them.

Will looks toward shore but keeps paddling. Then, just as we're almost around the last point before Granne's, just as we're almost out of sight, we hear them calling to us.

"Hey, Greeny! Guys!"

Will's ahead of me and I see him turn his head and look, then eyes forward.

And then he stops paddling, looks over his shoulder at me and says, so quietly that his voice won't carry over the water to them on the shore, "Did you want to stop in and see who's there?"

Do I?

"Not really." I shrug. "I mean, *scones.*"

He laughs and waves once at the people on the beach, and gets back to paddling.

I can hear their voices, though. Not what they're saying but their voices. Drifting out across the water as we disappear around the point. People talking.

# Parking lot

The rain starts overnight. I have to get up in the dark to close my window because the curtains are flapping around like flags and the rain is beating through the screen.

Back in bed, I listen to rain pounding the windows as if the storm is hurling stones at the house. I don't sleep well. Maybe I don't sleep at all.

Which means the perfect calm of last night's kayak expedition with Will, and the good feelings from the after-party, eating fresh scones with homemade jam at his kitchen table, listening to his mom and dad tell stories about what a goof my dad was in high school—"Remember that time Andy tried out for the school play, Billy? And he started arguing with Mrs. Langille about the words to that soliloquy from Hamlet?" "And he was right, wasn't he?"— is gone, all gone.

I do not feel calm. I do not feel right as I move carefully

around the kitchen, making toast and sipping juice, and trying not to let Granne see that the storm is everywhere around and inside me this morning.

And it really is everywhere. I've been texting my dad for three days and getting back these quick, totally meaningless replies.

Getting some things done here. Will check in soon. xo

Hope all well there on the point. Will be in touch soon. xo

Don't worry about me. Call you soon. xo

I know something's going on with my mom, but clearly he doesn't want to tell me yet.

Waiting for news sucks. Waiting for what will probably be bad news sucks even worse. So there's that.

"Let's pick up coffee at the bakery this morning," says Granne as we head into town for another morning of café prep. The furniture is supposed to arrive today or tomorrow, so we're going to stock the bookshelves today. Becca is supposed to come by and get Billy to help her hang some of her rugs as well, now that the painting is all done in the main room. "Maybe some cookies or cinnamon buns, too. It's just that kind of day," she adds, windshield wipers going. "Why don't you wait in the car, Larkin. I'll bring you a coffee, too. Or would you prefer tea?"

"Coffee, thanks." Yes, staying in the car is a good idea because I don't feel like talking to anyone, making eye contact, smiling politely. You know, doing normal social interactions with people in a public space. Here in the car with the radio playing softly, wipers going—yes, that suits me just fine.

But as soon as Granne dashes up the stairs and into the bakery, there's a sharp knock on the window beside me.

It's Beth. Casey's stink-eye Beth, who I've seen maybe three times in all since I've been here, mostly from a distance.

She's standing there in a raincoat with the hood up and is clearly waiting for me to open the window.

"Hi," she says when I finally get around to it. Granne's car is old and the power window button is hard to find. Beth probably thinks I'm just being cranky.

"Hi."

"Just going in to help out," she nods toward the bakery. "Chels calls me sometimes when they're short-staffed in the morning 'cause my job at the drugstore doesn't start until one."

"Oh. Right." *And you're telling me all this, why?*

202

"So, yeah, I'm glad I ran into you, Larkin, 'cause I just wanted to mention," she says, and leans a little closer to the window opening, smelling of cigarettes and smiling a little as if we're friends. "That was you and Will last night, right? Kayaking?"

"Yeah."

"Yeah, well, just so you know. You should be careful how much you hang out with Will."

Long pause, while I try to process what she just said. My tired, storm-messed-up brain isn't getting it at all.

"I know you think he's all cool and nice and everything," Beth continues, with her eyes trying to pin me to some imaginary wall. She's also smiling a little, a *sorry I'm the one to tell you this smile.* I have seen this same smile on people I know at home: *So I hate to tell you this, but I heard this girl talking, and she said you and Jonah* ... "But I know Will really, really well because we went out for over a year, and he's a bit messed up, you know? Like his dad?"

"Messed up like his dad?" I say, but actually I'm just trying to process that Will went out with this girl for a year. Really? How did *that* happen?

Beth's getting into it now that I've responded. I'm confused, still trying to picture her and Will going out together, so her words aren't registering. I'm also having flashbacks of me in my darkened room, and Amanda telling me what Jasmine heard Sunni say after that thing happened …

"Yeah, you know. Like how Mr. Greenfield was such a drunk for so many years—everybody knows that—and how he burned Henwoods' shed down."

I'm trying to understand but I also want her to shut up. "I've never seen Will drink. Or smoke."

Now she's getting to it. She wants to be the one telling the bad news. She wants to be the one to cause trouble, pain. I know people like this, so I shouldn't believe a thing she says, but she keeps talking and I'm trapped there in the car.

"I'm sorry, Larkin," she says and I know she's not but, yup, I keep listening. "Will was pretty awful to me when we were going out."

"Awful?"

"Oh, yes. He has some issues, you know, like his dad. I know it looks like he controls it really well, and all the teachers and everyone think he's great, but I'm just saying, speaking from experience, be careful. I was the new girl and he kind of hit on me. And now," she shrugs, "it's you. Know what I mean?"

Becca's voice in the car—*Will's such a sweetie*. Granne calling him "William" and giving him advice about special programs at Dal. Suzanne, and her eyes on her son yesterday at the café when she brought him the mail.

All the teachers and everyone. *Jonah Parker-Li, top athlete award. Jonah Parker-Li, school leadership award …*

"So he, like, hit you? Or what?" I feel like I'm swimming and can't get my breath, can't touch bottom.

"Well, no, he didn't hit me," she says, shrugging a little, backtracking maybe. "But he gets all quiet sometimes when he's mad, and then he gets really angry. You can hear it in his voice. He made me feel scared and not safe, to be honest. So we broke up."

She waits for me to say something and I don't, because I'm still trying to process it. I should be saying, "You're a liar," because I think she is, but part of me is asking why she's telling me this. And part of me is thinking that I've heard Will's voice change, too.

"And Casey, he could see what was going on, so he sort of rescued me, you could say."

"Casey." The local cool guy who hosts drinking parties at the family fire pit.

Beth nods meaningfully at me. She really wants to get into it now, I can tell. Casey Henwood, her knight in shining armor.

*Yeah, so maybe you should be careful around Beth and Casey.*

"He asked me out and Will was super mad, but he didn't want to get into it with Casey, because I guess they've known each other for so long, so he just went away," she says. "Until you came."

He came over the point in the dark and said, "Hey," and then came another night and we talked about how Harry Potter makes me cry. The kayaks. The seals. I told him about swimming to Prince Edward Island. I told him about my mother. *Seafoam.*

Beth leans in, bringing her cigarette smell even closer and says in a low voice, "And apart from Will, there's his dad. Of course, you know what happened with the fire at the café, right …?"

"Good morning, Beth," says Granne, opening the car door. Did she hear? Apparently not. "Here, take these, Larkin." She hands me my coffee and a bag of what must be cinnamon buns and slides in.

"Oh, hello, Mrs. Day." Beth, being all polite to the old lady retired school principal, smiling now that her storytelling is done. "Just having a chat with Larkin before heading in to help Chelsea." Beth, just a nice girl, standing in the rain, chatting with a friend.

"Good girl, because Chelsea can use the help," says Granne. "It's very busy in there this morning."

"It must be the rain," says Beth. Good little Beth. "I'd better go. Bye! Bye, Larkin—maybe we'll see you at the back shore next time Casey has a bonfire."

Granne waits for me to say something, but I'm still stunned into silence, unable to form words. "Bye." She says it for us both.

And then she pushes the button on her side to roll up my window and looks across at me.

"All right, Larkin?"

"Yeah, fine."

I take a shaky sip of coffee as I watch Beth go up the steps of the bakery and turn to give us a little wave before disappearing inside.

# Broken

"She's an odd duck, that Beth McAdam," says Granne as she unlocks the café door. She's fishing, I know. But I don't bite.

I don't bite because my head is already starting to hum. Beth's words are chasing around, and there I am trying to catch them and understand. She's warning me about Will.

No one warned me about Jonah. Maybe it all would have been different if someone—some girl or even some boy—had said, "You know, Larkin, he can be a real dick. He drinks. He does drugs. Everyone thinks he's so good and smart and perfect, but he does bad stuff, too. Watch out. Be careful."

That's not what people said, though. Not the girls, anyway. They said he was hot. (Like, no kidding. Jonah Parker-Li could be a model. An underwear model. Honestly.) He wins academic awards. He's a star athlete. Yes, he hangs with those cool jock boys and that whole crowd of kids with perfect skin, great hair, and their own cars. But he's a good student, too, and speaks at assemblies about volunteering as a coach with the kids from that tough neighborhood. A role model. I mean, how are you supposed to know this is a guy who can also get you drunk, lead you to his car, and hurt you?

You're supposed to know because someone warns you. Even if it's someone standing in the rain and leaning in your car window, breathing cigarette fumes on you as she tells you stuff that you don't want to believe.

"So let's get a couple of shelves filled and see what it looks like," Granne is saying, and I nod and take another sip of my coffee so that she can't see the messy stuff that must be written all over my face. Force myself to move to the storage room, pick up the box marked "Mysteries," and get to work.

Work helps for a while. Even when work means books.

My mother loves books—*loved* books? I don't know if she reads anymore, but my childhood memories are of books everywhere. Stacked beside her bed. Stacked beside mine (and they had to be in the right order for bedtime reading, with favorites on the bottom so they'd be the last thing I thought about as I drifted off to sleep). Trips to the library with Mom. That's where we were coming from that day the guy ran a red light and ruined everything.

So, books on shelves. Alphabetical by author. Patterson. Penny. Rankin. Robinson. I lift them out and set them, spines out, in order. It's mechanical and soothing, and slowly I come back to myself. I notice stuff again, like that Granne has turned on the CD player in the corner and something classical is playing. A clarinet and an orchestra. I must have lifted my head, like a dog with its nose in the air, sniffing, on the trail of something, because Granne says, "It's Mozart. Good music to work to, I think."

She doesn't look at me as she says it. She's over at the other wall, taking children's books out of bags and lining them up on the shelves.

"I like it," I say, not looking at her, either. "You're right. It's good music to work to."

So we work like that for a while and the air calms down around me and inside me. I still see Beth's face and I still hear echoes of her words, but they're going through the processor now, not so loud and harsh. Books in my hands. Books from the box to the shelves.

Books are calming me down, which, let's face it, is kind of a miracle.

Billy arrives, and he and Granne move into the kitchen to

talk dishwashers and plumbing. I glance at him and look for whatever Beth thinks his issues are, but all I see is his swaying walk and his little sideways smile as he passes me. So I stick with my books, going back to the storage room to grab another box or bag, and check my phone, which I've left on the table there, hoping there's something from Dad.

On the third trip, there is.

Call me when you can xo

I can hear Granne and Billy in the kitchen, and now they've moved to the back door and are going onto the back porch. I hear "downspout" and "rain barrel" as I call.

It must be very early in the morning there, but he picks it up on the first ring. "Lark?"

"Hi, Dad."

"Hi, honey. You got my text. Glad you called."

"So, what's up?"

"First, everything okay there? You're good?"

"Dad, I'm good. What's up? Come on."

"Well, it's this." And then he doesn't say anything for a long time and I know something bad is coming because I can hear him swallowing, over and over. Getting ready to talk.

When Granne and Billy come back in, I'm out on the front porch, sitting on a step stool, one of those little plastic ones that kids use at the bathroom sink so they can reach the taps. It's robin's egg blue. I think how funny it is that you register small details like that when your brain is being battered by bad stuff.

Mom is not going to be coming home, Dad tells me. Ever. The doctors say she is brain-damaged, that she'll never be able to function at a safe level again. She has to stay in a hospital or care home forever and her life expectancy has been compromised—that's the word Dad uses—by the drug use and other things that have happened to her.

I ask, what things? And after another long pause, he tells me about the police in Vancouver and Seattle, and as far away as San Francisco, finding her beaten or bleeding or incoherent on the street more than once, between rehab sessions. He says the brain injuries on top of the drug use were too much, and how she slips in and out of a catatonic stupor. He says my grandparents are devastated, but they understand there's nothing more that can be done. My mom, their daughter, Dad's wife, is never going to be well, is never going to come home.

"I'm flying out tonight, Lark. I'll go home first to get the car and I'll be there Friday night, okay?"

"Okay. Good."

He doesn't say anything about Lynette, so I hope she's not part of the plan. I'm not sure I could handle Lynette right now.

"It's not great news, Lark. I'm sorry."

"It's okay." He sounds awful and I don't know how to help him. "It's not your fault, Dad."

Fault. It would be so much easier if I could blame someone for everything.

"Is Granne there?"

She is. She's standing right beside me. I don't even know how long she's been standing here.

"Yeah, she's here. Do you want to talk to her?"

"Yes, please. And Lark … hang in there … okay? I'll be there soon. Call or text me any time, day or night, okay?" Dad's starting to sound a bit panicky now. Time to bail.

"Here's Granne. Love you."

I hand her my phone and stand up. Return to my books. Feel nothing.

# *Mail*

When Granne returns my phone, she asks me to run over to the post office and pick up her mail. Maybe she wants to give me some time and space on my own. Or maybe it's just that the tables and chairs might be delivered today and she doesn't want to go out. Maybe a bit of both.

"Sure. Now?" I'm so relieved she doesn't mention the call with my dad.

"Yes, please. Maybe finish that last shelf and go."

The shelves look great. Actually, they looked great even without books on them, because Billy is a woodworking wiz. He stained the wood dark brown, and the edges are softly rounded. Their end pieces (whatever you call them in woodworking—I don't have a clue) are a bit swirly, so the last book on the shelf kind of peeks over if you look at it from the end.

"Very classy, Billy," Granne tells him and he smiles, for once.

214

"You've got a very classy place here, Mrs. D."

The post office is just across the street and I know its steps very well, after spending most of that Friday night there a couple of weeks ago, watching the café burn. I've never been inside, though. The woman behind the counter knows all about me, apparently, because she asks how things are coming along and do I know when the café will be open, and won't it be great to have a place to go to get a cup of coffee and be surrounded by books.

"Closing the library, honestly, you have to wonder what the County was thinking," she says, handing me a bundle of envelopes. "Thank goodness for people like Anne Day."

"Yes." I glance down at the envelopes and see one addressed to me in unfamiliar handwriting.

*Larkin Day, c/o Mrs. Day, Tuttle Harbour …*

And written in block letters in the lower left corner: CONFIDENTIAL.

Crazy way to address an envelope. I mean, it's not even an address, really. But someone knows where I'm staying, obviously. Someone is writing to me. Confidentially.

I'm standing outside on the post office steps when I open it and read the typed page, and immediately wish I hadn't.

*Hey Larkin,*

*Amanda gave me your address. I get that you're upset about what happened, but you need to stop lying to people. We both know you're the one who was drunk and high and followed me around all night at Anil's party. And we both know nothing happened when you got into my car. You fell out and landed on your face when I opened the door for you. You were too drunk to remember anything.*

*Maybe you should think about changing schools next year, because everyone knows that you're lying and it's going to be pretty awkward for you at Bayview. Amanda and Jasmine think so, too.*

*I know you have a lot of bad stuff happening in your life right now* (my mother, he means. Amanda must have told him about my mother, too) *so maybe it's time for you to move on and start fresh somewhere else.*

*Good luck.*

*Jonah Parker-Li*

I find myself sitting on the post office steps again, and I can't tell if it's the middle of the night or a gray and misty noon hour. Also, I feel slightly nauseated and there's a hum in my head. I close my eyes and lean forward so that my head is resting on my folded arms. That's what you're supposed to do when you're going to faint, right? When all the blood is rushing out of your head?

"Larkin?"

I raise my head too quickly and see sparkles around the dark edges of my vision.

Becca Patriquin is leaning toward me, looking worried. She reaches out to touch my shoulder, to keep me from tilting sideways, I think.

"Can I help you?"

I try to say something like, "No, I'm fine." Try to focus on her face, on those piercing blue-gray eyes, which I suddenly realize are the same color as the water last night when Will and I were kayaking. Try to speak but, when I do, I embarrass myself completely by starting to cry. And I don't even care now.

*You need to stop lying to people.*

"Come with me, Larkin. Here," she says, handing me a tissue.

She helps me stand up (oh, God, everyone's going to see the

freaking-out girl from a few weeks ago freaking out again, and I don't even care right now) and I drop the mail.

"I'll get it."

"No!" I don't want her to read it. I don't want anyone to read it.

But she beats me to it. While I stand and wobble on the post office steps, she scoops up the envelopes and the one sheet of paper and hands them to me. My hands are shaking so much I can't even fold Jonah's letter and put it back in its envelope.

"Larkin, let me." And I'm just so shaky and lost and deafened by the humming in my head that I let her. I don't even try to stop her when I see her eyes land on the first paragraph. Read and register.

But she doesn't say anything. She just folds the letter, slips it back into the envelope and hands it back to me.

"Come on. I'm headed to the café," she says in a perfectly normal voice. "I'll walk back with you."

We don't talk at all, which is fine with me, because I don't think I could form my own words right now. All I can hear are Jonah's.

*You need to stop lying to people ...*

We walk. I still feel a bit sick but I don't think I'm going to faint. It's only when we get to the steps of the café porch that I realize Becca's hand has been under my elbow the whole way across the street. I hadn't even noticed that she was guiding me until I feel her let go.

# On the shore, again

I survived the rest of the day. Most of the books are now placed on shelves. Becca and Billy carefully hang her rugs on the walls. The tables and chairs don't arrive and Granne makes phone calls to sort it out. Will comes in and picks up on the fact that I'm not very talkative and he just turns to his work, and I feel frozen and tight around him.

So I'm now on the shore, watching the sun drop out of the clearing clouds and throw its streamers of light across the sandbars. I'm calculating the distance to Prince Edward Island. Again.

Mom. No. I'm not even going think about that now. I need Dad beside me when I go there.

But the other stuff, the letter from Jonah, so full of lies and maybe even threats, I don't know. And Beth and her insider info. Yeah, Beth. And Will.

Beth is a lightweight, probably even a liar, I know that. I

know girls just like her, back home at Bayview Collegiate. But her words have stayed with me, just like Jonah's. Words do that. Words spoken and words in books. Words you write. They start to breathe and live and just take over. And right now, I've been taken over by the words of other people—people talking—and I can't find myself or my own words.

So I'm testing myself a bit. If Will comes over the point tonight, I'm going to ask him straight out: *Did you go out with Beth for a year and scare her away?*

He doesn't come across the point. But something catches my eye down the shore, someone walking toward me from the direction of Granne's house.

Chelsea. She waves when she sees that I've noticed her.

"I was looking for you," she calls across the drying seaweed to where I sit in my little sandy cove near the end of the beach. She's wearing a bathing suit and cutoffs, with a beach towel draped around her shoulders like a shawl. Going swimming. Here?

"Looking for me?"

She drops her towel on the sand and sits beside me.

"Fire on the back shore tonight. Beth texted me that we should come over," she says.

*We should come over.* Me. Beth wants me to come. Probably has more fun stuff to share with me.

"Yeah, I don't know," I say and shrug. Hopefully she'll pick up on my lack of enthusiasm and move on.

Chelsea is all legs and skinny arms and red hair. I mean, *red* hair. Fire-engine red. Canadian flag red. Her towel is a blinding combination of fluorescent stripes. She's pretty spectacular in the color department, especially here on the shore, with the sun setting and the red (no, a different red) sand and the blue water reflecting the lilac streaks from the sky. I can't help smiling at her.

"Yes, you do," she says. "Come on."

She's patient, that's for sure. She just waits while we sit there, watching the sun get bigger as it drops toward the water.

"I've had a crap day," I say finally. "I'm not sure I'm up to facing all those guys."

"Yeah, I get that. About crap days. I have a lot of those, too."

I glance at her but she's just watching the sunset, smiling a little. I think her red hair must be her statement: *I'm ignoring you all and doing what I want.* I wish I could be like that. I think maybe I was, once, when I was younger. When school was still fun and I didn't know the whole story about my mother. I'm not anymore, though. Now I just weep over books and take any available route to oblivion whenever offered.

"They're not that bad," she says suddenly. "You know, Casey and Beth and them. They're okay if you just kind of take them for what they are."

Hmmm. Right. "What are they, then?"

She laughs. "Good question. Well, Casey's kind of the boss."

I can see that. "Okay. What about Beth?"

"His minion?"

We both laugh at that.

"Yeah, I'm not sure she's a minion," I say. No way. She's someone who makes things happen, which is why she tapped on the car window this morning and told me her little story.

"No, you're right. She more of a—I don't know—a stage manager or something … you know what I mean?" Chelsea shakes her head.

I want to ask her about Beth and Will, about whether it was actually a thing, whether what Beth said this morning could even be true, but I don't. I'm not sure I want to know.

No, I don't want to know. Not yet. Avoid.

"What about those two guys, Vin? And Mike?"

"Mick. Vin and Mick," she laughs. "They're not brothers but they might as well be. They live just up the Gulf Shore. Next-door neighbors. Farm boys. Interested in only two things—baseball and machines with four wheels and an engine. Oh, and cows, of course. They're nice," she adds. "They're both crap at school, but even the teachers like them."

In other words, harmless.

So that leaves Will, but I'm not going to say his name because I don't really want to hear what Chelsea's capsule version of him is. I've heard too many versions of him already.

Chelsea can't read my mind, though.

"And then there's Will," she says, turning to me. "But of course, you know all about him."

I don't, actually.

"Yeah."

"Nice guy." She nods. "The nicest."

That's hopeful. Chelsea knows Will. Maybe I should just ask her about him and Beth, about Beth's story today in the rainy bakery parking lot, but the moment passes before I can fit the words together, and Chelsea has already moved on.

"So? Are we going to this fire, or what?" she asks. "Come on. I need a swim. And I have my mom's car so we can drive up the farm lane beside Henwoods' cow pasture. No climbing over the rocks. Come on. You need some fun." She elbows me. "I promise I'll stick to Coke and make you do the same." Which is nice of her to say, considering that she's already seen me in action with this crowd.

"Okay, I guess." Sounds safe enough.

"Come on. Let's do this," she says in a sporty cheerleader voice, hauling me up off the sand.

She helps me shake out the damp quilt and we make our way down the shore toward Granne's, while she tells me about some lady who showed up at the bakery today, asking for some impossible number of molasses cookies. Or something. I force myself to laugh, listen, try to sound as if I'm paying attention.

I'm not, of course. I'm somewhere in the clouds, thinking about Will and Beth, thinking about my mother—no, not thinking about my mother. Jonah Parker-Li and his words about lying. Back to Beth saying, "He made me feel scared and not safe, to be honest."

I just want it to stop, so this is better than spending the evening with Granne watching me for cracks to open up. Or worse, wanting to talk.

No, Chelsea and I will go to the fire on the back shore because Will isn't coming over the point tonight to sit with me on the quilt and explain it all.

But that doesn't stop me from looking over my shoulder a few times to scan the empty beach, hoping to see his silhouette against the sky.

# The cat pounces

"Hey! You finally made it!"

Casey goes all party host when Chelsea and I get out of her mom's little car and walk across the grass to join the small group standing around the campfire. For some reason, sitting in chairs isn't a thing here, I've noticed. Maybe because that would mean someone would actually have to bring chairs. Maybe it's just that standing makes it easy to move around, change the mix, run into the waves. Which is exactly what Chelsea is doing right now.

"Finally! I need a swim. Now!" And she's gone, dropping her towel, scrambling out of her cut-offs, running down the bank and over the sand to where the waves are lapping in over the near sandbar.

"Wait! We're in!" Vin and Mick are peeling off T-shirts to follow her, as if they've been waiting.

"Hi, Larkin," Mick calls to me as the two of them—no, not

brothers, but Chelsea's right; they might as well be—lope after her.

Which leaves me standing there on my own with Casey and Beth.

Minion. No. She's more like a cat, Beth. There's a cup of something in her hand and she slinks close to Casey and presses up against his side, under his arm, eyes fixed on me the whole time. I can almost see a tail twitching. She takes a sip and watches me. Purring.

Casey doesn't seem to mind Beth doing her possession thing on him. He's holding a cup, too. He doesn't offer me anything, because he's probably scared of Granne after the last time.

"So how did Chelsea convince you?" he asks me.

*Well, I sat on the shore, hoping Will would come over the point so we could talk about some stuff that has me worried, and that didn't happen, and Chelsea appeared and suggested this. So, yeah. Here I am.*

"Well, I had a crap day, and this sounded better than sitting at home watching my grandmother work on her spreadsheets," I say out loud. Better. Keeping it light. I don't look at Beth when I say this, because I don't really want to show her how big a part of my crap day she is.

"Opening day, eh? Still coming soon? Even after the fire?" Casey seems interested. Beth has gone all still, but it feels to me as if her cat tail is still swishing.

"Yup. Sometime next week, we hope." Time for a new topic. I wave my hand out toward the water. "So, Chelsea's a bit of a water baby, eh?"

Casey laughs at that. "Always. She's the first one in every time. And it doesn't matter how cold it is, either."

"She's a fish," says Beth. "Or a seal, maybe. Have you been in yet?"

"No, I'm a wuss about the water here. You know, all that seaweed and stuff you can feel with your feet," I say. Yes, I'm revealing my urban Ontario feebleness, but I don't care. Also, it means I can sidestep any mention of those fading bruises on my legs.

"Ha, you really are a wuss. Come on, Larkin," says Beth, and she slinks out from under Casey's arm and puts her drink down on the grass and peels off her tank top to reveal a bikini top. "You need to get into the water at least once."

"No, thanks." What is she doing? Now it's the cut-offs.

"Come on, Larkin. You've been out on the kayaks with Will.

229

We've seen you. Next step, into the water. Are you wearing your bathing suit? Come on, peel off."

She's being so weird that I feel the hum start in my head. Her joking, don't-be-a-wuss voice has an edge that Casey hears, too. Also the striptease act.

"Hey, lay off," he says. "If Larkin doesn't want to swim, it's not a big deal."

Beth leaves her clothes in a pile, picks up her cup, and takes a long drink. "And there he is. Casey to the rescue."

She's drunk. She has to be. The hum in my head is getting louder, and I realize all at once that coming here tonight was the worst decision ever and I need to go. Back to the house. Back to Granne and her spreadsheets.

"Are you okay?" Casey looks at me as if he thinks I'm sick. Maybe I am sick. My hands are shaking and I jam them into my pockets.

"I'm okay but, you know, I think maybe I should just go home." Before the hum gets any louder, before Beth can say anything else. I glance at her and she's smirking at me.

"I'll just get Chelsea," I say and look out at the water. She's pretty far out now, too far to call to. Shit.

"Hey, I'll drive you back," says Casey, and he puts his drink down, comes toward me, and puts his hand on my back as if I need guiding or holding up. I jump a little and Beth notices.

"Casey, she doesn't need your help."

"No, really, it's okay. I can walk back. It's not dark yet and I'll just follow the lane," I say, trying to get away from them.

"Larkin, I'm driving you back. It's okay, it was just Coke," he says, nodding over at the cup he just put down, and I feel his hand on my back again as he guides me to the ATV, parked back on the grass away from the fire. I want to shake him off because it feels too much like something that happened once before. When? Oh, right. But I also know I really need to get out of here, soon.

"You're falling for her act, Casey," calls Beth. "Just like Will did."

We both turn and look at her. When did Will come into this? I'm about to ask her, but Casey starts moving us toward the ATV again.

"Beth, just drop it, eh? I'll be right back," he says. "Don't go in the water, either. You might drown."

"Ha, as if you care," Beth says, but she doesn't move to stop us now. The tail isn't switching around; the purring is silent. Now she just stands there in her bathing suit and sways a little. Yes, drunk.

Casey and I are at the ATV now. It has small doors and a sort of roll-bar roof thing, and it feels enclosed and small, so I climb in and huddle a bit toward my side, hoping he doesn't want to chat much. It's so noisy once we get rolling, and a bit rough, so I concentrate on counting and breathing, while holding tight to the frame to steady me over the bumps in the lane.

And then he stops. Just before the bend in the lane, at a spot where they can't see us from the shore, and the road is still out of sight around the curve of the lane. Basically, in the middle of nowhere, in the gathering dark. Shadowy cow pasture on one side, forest of dense bush on the other.

"What are you doing?" I ask. My voice is coming from somewhere outside my body because I'm not even sure who I am right now.

"I just wanted to tell you something," he says, turning to me.

"Take me home please," I whisper, eyes forward.

"No, listen, Larkin. I have to tell you something and I didn't want Beth to be around."

I can't breathe now. My hands reach for the door, scrabble

around, trying to figure out how to open the stupid little door on my side. It's nothing like Jonah's car but it feels the same, even with the sky right there above us, and no windows, no back seat. My fingers can't find the door handle. It's on the outside, maybe, and I try to stand up. Maybe I can just climb over the side, but now Casey grabs my arm and is pulling at me to sit down, trying to pull me around to face him, but I can't look at him. I'm trying to get the stupid door open, and I just know there are going to be bruises.

"Larkin! Listen, I just wanted to tell you something. About the fire. About Beth. Larkin, relax! Stop!"

It's happening again. I can't breathe. I try to speak, to call out for help, to tell him to let go of me.

"I'm not going to hurt you," Casey says, putting one arm around my shoulders to hold me still in my seat, and I want to believe him because he sounds a bit scared, too.

And then a vehicle, a truck, swings around the curve of the road from behind the scrubby trees and stops in front of us, still running.

The headlights pick us up as if Casey and I are center stage. His arm around my shoulder, our heads close together. Both of us squinting into the sudden spotlight.

"Hey, Will!" Casey calls, and lets go of me as I push him away. I have to find the door. I have to get to Will.

Will sits there behind the wheel—I can just see him in the truck cab beyond the screaming headlights—staring at us. And as I push Casey away and try to figure out how to open this stupid door, he swings the truck around in a big U-turn and drives away.

A few heartbeats of silence, and then Casey says, "That was weird. What's his problem?"

"Just take me home," I manage to whisper. Stupid door still closed. I give up.

"Okay. All right." He sounds tired, fed up with me, and I huddle over on my side, arms wrapped around myself, trying to stop shaking.

After that, Casey doesn't say anything more until he drops me at the bottom of the deck stairs.

"Hey, I'm sorry if I scared you, Larkin," he says. "I was just trying to help."

"Just go," I whisper. It's all I can manage. I have no breath, and the world is one enormous humming, spinning bubble, as I finally figure out how to get the door open and almost fall out. My feet feel unstable on the ground and I stumble away from him.

He waits a moment, then turns the ATV around, gunning the engine, and drives away, as I use all my concentration to climb up the stairs, slide the door open, and stumble into the kitchen where Granne is waiting.

# *Drifting*

I feel the quilt pulling tight over me as Granne sits down on the side of my bed. Sort of like a hug. It reminds me of being little, when Mom would come to tuck me in. Mom, and then Dad. That cozy safe feeling.

I didn't even close my bedroom door after the hot bath that Granne ran for me, after I pulled on pajama pants and a sweatshirt because I was still shivering, after I climbed into bed. Closing the door was too much work. I could hear the kettle and the clink of the teapot lid, the spoon in the sugar bowl (twice—three times), the spoon stirring the tea in the mug. When I hear her coming down the hall, I can't even roll over to face her.

She puts the tea down on my bedside table and lowers herself to sit on the edge, close to my back so that the covers pull around me, swaddling me. That's what they do to babies, right? That's me. Swaddled in sheets and quilt. A baby again.

"I've brought you some tea," she says.

"Thank you," I whisper, but it's muffled by the pillow that my face is jammed into.

Granne puts her hand on my head then, smoothing my hair the way my mom used to. Maybe this is a universal mom thing, because Granne does it perfectly. Forehead, temple, behind the ear, a little more pressure toward the neck as she smooths my hair down. Lifts her hand. Starts again.

Tears seep out from my closed eyes, but at least I'm not shivering anymore.

After a while, she rests her hand on my head, then my shoulder. Gives me a pat.

"I'll leave you now, Larkin," she says. "Unless you want to talk?"

Talking. Last thing I feel like doing right now. Not sure I can even form the words to describe what's going on inside my head.

"Maybe later," I manage to say into the pillow.

"Later, then. I'll be up for a while. If you want to talk, I'll be here. I'll leave your door open a little and you just have to call. I'll hear you."

She stands up and the bed creaks a little. I hear her move off down the hall, the clink of the tea pot spout on the edge of a mug and the metallic tinkle of the spoon, fridge door opening and closing, the kitchen chair scraping across the floor as she sits down.

Then, a sigh. A deep sigh.

A few more tears leak out but I'm not shivering now. I'm empty. It's as if everything has drained out of my head, out of my heart, too. Mom. And Dad. And Jonah Parker-Li's awful letter, and Beth with her hints about Will. Casey trying to be nice but just scaring me so much, and Will turning and driving away from us. What's real, what isn't real, what happened, what really happened, people talking ...

I'm too tired. Too empty. I feel waves washing over me like the waves on the shore. They carry me off into some watery depth where it's quiet and I'm alone. All the voices go away. All the people go away, and I want them to go. I just want to drift here.

Drift. Maybe drift all the way to Seafoam.

# Messages

I sleep through the rest of Wednesday night and half of Thursday. Get up to go to the bathroom and take a long drink of water from the glass Granne leaves on my bedside table—that mug of tea magically disappeared at some point—climb back into bed and sleep until late afternoon. I hear rain slapping against the window and burbling in the downspout at the corner of the house. Raindrops tapping on the grass.

No. I'm not hungry. Granne checks on me before leaving for town. "I'll lock the doors and no one will bother you, Larkin ... just sleep as long as you want ... I'll be home later this afternoon" I mumble a response. A nod against the pillow.

"Okay."

I sleep. It's as if I haven't slept for months and need to catch up, which might be true. Or it's not sleep at all, but more of a deep dive into a socially acceptable place where I don't have to see anyone, talk to anyone, think about anything, imagine anything. I don't even remember if I dream. I sleep, and that's all.

But eventually I do wake up, roll over, and stare at the ceiling. The ancient clock radio beside my bed says 4:18. Am I hungry? No. Thirsty? Not really. Okay? Yeah, I'm okay.

I reach for my phone to see if there are any messages from Dad—and realize that it's completely out of power. If he's been trying to reach me ...

That's enough to get me moving. First thing, plug in my phone. I get up and shuffle off to the kitchen with my charger.

Just boarding. Will text you when I land.

Landed in Toronto.

Two texts from last night. And just a few hours ago:

Home. Will leave first thing tomorrow. Hope to be there by midnight at the latest.

You there, Lark?

I text him that I've been sick with some bug (well, I have to call it something, right?) and didn't charge my phone, but I'm up and okay now, just waiting for Granne to get home from town. Supper. All normal. All good.

He calls a few seconds later and I think about letting it go to voicemail, but that would just delay everything, so I don't.

"Hey, Lark, are you okay? Feeling better?"

"Yeah, I'm okay now. Just slept it off." I try to sound hearty, but I'm pretty sure I fail. "Are you okay?"

"I'm doing okay. Just tired. Just sad. Really missing you."

*Don't make me cry, Dad. Don't make me cry, please …*

He must take my silence as a warning because he changes direction then.

"So, I'm just getting a few things organized here at the house, and I'll be hitting the road first thing tomorrow, early as I can. Before the sun's up, probably. Which means I can be there late tomorrow night. Okay?"

"Sounds good. If you're tired, get a hotel or something."

"Hey, I can do this trip in my sleep," he says and I can hear him smiling. "Done it so many times. Don't worry."

"Okay."

"Okay. Everything all right there? You're sure you're feeling better?"

"Everything's fine here." *Liar, liar, pants on fire.* But, oh well. "I'm feeling okay, just tired." Tired? After sleeping almost eighteen hours?

I hear the front door open and lean around the kitchen doorway to see Granne coming in. She catches sight of me on the phone and mouths, "Your father?"

"Granne just got home from town. Do you want to talk to her?"

"Sure, I can fill her in on the plans."

She comes into the kitchen and I hand over my phone, still plugged in.

"Andrew. We'll see you tomorrow?"

Travel plans. Timing. ETA and all that. I tune out and get up to stare out the kitchen window at the waves being driven in over the sandbars, wild and rough with the rainstorm. The water is red with sand, and clumps of slimy seaweed lie in a line along the shore, carried in with the tide now that everything is churned up.

Granne's home phone rings, startling both of us.

"There's construction on the Trans-Canada at Fredericton," she says to Dad, while pointing at the portable kitchen phone that sits on the little desk in the corner and waving vaguely toward me. She wants me to answer, gives me a look.

Okay, it might be important. Maybe something to do with the delivery of appliances next week or something, so fine, I'll answer it for her.

The call display says *Henry Burgess* and a local number.

"Hello?"

"Hey, is that you, Larkin?"

I know this voice.

"Hi, yeah. Chelsea?"

"Yes, it's me. Listen … I just wanted to check that you're okay. After last night—I don't know what happened exactly, but Casey came back and was kind of upset."

Oh, great. I glance at Granne, point at myself, and mouth, "Chelsea," so she waves and turns back to talking to Dad. I move into the living room where she won't be able to hear.

"Yeah, well, it was a bit weird, but I'm okay. And Casey doesn't need to be upset. He didn't do anything."

Well, not really, anyway. He just stopped driving in the middle of dark nowhere and scared the shit out of me. And then made it look as if he and I were into something, sending Will U-turning into oblivion.

"I think he was mostly mad at Beth, actually. But I'm glad you're okay. Sorry I was still out in the water or I could have driven you home." She sounds genuinely sorry, which kind of hurts a bit because she's being so nice to me, and it didn't even occur to me to call and explain why I left the back shore without her.

"I've actually been sleeping off some bug ever since or I would have called to apologize," I tell her. White lie, but it'll do.

"No worries at all," she says. "But listen, there's something I wanted to tell you. Something Beth said last night."

Beth again. Do I really want to hear anything that Beth has to say?

"It's important," Chelsea says, as if she's reading my mind.

"Larkin." Granne is suddenly beside me, holding out my now unplugged and partly charged phone with the unspoken message: *Your father wants to talk you again.*

"Chelsea, I have to go now—my dad's calling on my cell." Damn.

"How about I pick you up after supper and we go get ice cream on Water Street," she says quickly. "Would that be okay?"

"Great. Let's do that. See you then. Bye."

I'm distracted now. *Something Beth said last night.* Dad and I talk a little bit longer about nothing much. There's not much to say.

"Miss you, Lark. I'm looking forward to seeing you."

"Me, too, Dad."

"And don't wait up, okay? Not sure when I'll get there, and you don't have to stay up."

"I'll probably stay up, but yeah, okay. I'll leave you a welcome note if I can't keep my eyes open."

"Perfect."

We talk like this for another minute, as if he doesn't want to hang up and get back to (what did he call it?) organizing the house. Maybe organizing Lynette, I don't know. But finally we sign off and after a minute of staring out the living room window, and taking a few deep breaths while counting to five, to ten, to fifteen, and closing my eyes and trying to picture my dad's face, I head back to the kitchen.

"I'm going to grill us some chicken for supper," Granne says. I hadn't noticed that she'd brought groceries with her from the Co-op. "Salad, and some lovely fresh new potatoes here."

"Sounds great."

"You're hungry?" She gives me a teacher look, assessing my ability to eat, maybe, so I nod. "Good. Here, you can wash the lettuce."

I get started pulling greens apart and washing them at the sink, and she takes over the counter with her chicken breasts and spices. It's mindless busy-work. We don't talk as we putter together in the kitchen, as if everything is normal.

# On the road

Chelsea picks me up at six-thirty and we head down the road toward town.

"Oh, look. It's Will," she says, slowing down for the approaching familiar red pick-up truck and rolling down her window.

I want to tell her to keep driving, because all I can see is his face on Wednesday night, through the blare of headlights on the windscreen, then the silhouette of his head as he turns around and drives off, leaving me with Casey. I want to explain and I also don't want to talk about it. I want to see him but I don't want him to see me. I want to explain but I don't want him to ask.

In other words, I'm a mess. It probably shows, too.

"Hey, Will!" Chelsea doesn't notice this, though, because she's waving out the window so he'll stop and chat. I think for a second that he's just going to wave and keep going but, no, he probably doesn't notice me there in the passenger seat.

He slows to a stop, window to window, smiling hello.

Sees me.

There's a moment when we look at each other and I'm sure this whole conversation is taking place.

*What was that with you and Casey?*

*Nothing. It was nothing. He was scaring me.*

*I don't get it. I was coming to hang out and you were with Casey.*

*I wasn't. He was taking me home because Beth had been saying crazy stuff. She said crazy stuff about you. Is it true? Did you scare her? Should I be afraid of you?*

Will looks away from me, looks at Chelsea, but his face is closed now.

"Come with us." Chelsea hasn't heard the conversation, obviously. "We're going to get ice cream."

"Thanks, but no. Gotta get home." He's already moving back into driving position, glancing up the road toward his lane, then back at Chelsea. Avoiding me. "Sorry. Have fun."

"Oh, okay," says Chelsea as he drives off.

She watches the truck in the mirror for a minute, then she looks over at me.

I look straight ahead.

"Did you guys have a fight?" she says after a long pause. Starts driving up the road again.

"A fight? No. You make it sound like we're a couple or something." My voice isn't my voice.

"I don't know about the couple thing, but anyone could see, that first night he brought you to the back shore. You know, that *quite bad* night." She tries to sound like a teacher or a nanny or something, softening it by adding a little smile to the words. "And the kayaking. He likes you."

He likes me, and I thought I could trust him. Yes, okay, I like him, too.

Except it's all a mess now, thanks to Beth.

"Hey, you said you wanted to tell me something about Beth," I say, because the little flicker of whatever Chelsea ignited in me when she said those words seems like the most important thing in the world right now, and I want to fix this, fix everything. Well, maybe not everything. My mother cannot be fixed. Jonah Parker-Li cannot be fixed.

But Will—Will and me—maybe I can fix this.

"Right. Beth. Wait till I park."

We've made it into town and turn down one of the side

streets toward the harbor. Chelsea finds a parking spot near the old Knights Of Columbus Hall, which now houses a dairy bar with milkshakes and the *Best Ice Cream in Cumberland County* (as the sign says). Lots of people walking around now that the rain has moved off and the sky has cleared. Some kids are dancing around, pretending to put on a show on the stage in the park by the water. A lobster boat chugs up the channel toward the wharf across the harbor. The sun has broken through the clouds and is shooting rays into the puddles up and down Water Street.

I notice all this, but I'm impatient for Chelsea to park the stupid car and tell me about Beth.

"Ice cream first," she says.

"Fine." I must sound like a cranky five-year-old because Chelsea laughs at me.

But later, after we get our cones and start walking along the boardwalk that stretches between the harbor and the old fish plant, while we walk and lick and try to keep the melting French Vanilla (me) and Rocky Road (her) from dripping all over our hands, and Chelsea talks … later, I start to think—no, I start to believe—that there might be a way to change things. I might not have to drift off across the waves after all.

# Waiting

As soon as I see the light bloom like a cloud over the rise in the road, up near Becca's lane, and then the two bright pinpoints of headlights pop up over the little hill and get brighter and larger as they come down the road toward us, I stand up.

Dad.

I've been curled up, cannonball style, in one of the Muskoka chairs, with the beach quilt wrapped around me. Yes, it smells of seaweed. Yes, it's a bit sandy. But it makes me think of sitting on the shore with Will when we talked about Harry Potter and drifting off across the Strait. When I felt that things might be okay, at least for a while. So I've been sitting out here in the dark, cocooned in the quilt. Waiting.

Granne is here, too. She came out after supper with her wine and a book and has been quietly watching me—I know she's watching me, even though she's trying to hide it. I don't mind. She doesn't talk much, which is perfect.

"Herons are noisy tonight," she says, as three of them swoop over, enormous wings whooshing the air, squawking and sending the gulls in all directions.

"Mmmm. Yup." I watch them, crazy modern-day pterodactyls off to stand knee-deep in seaweed and fish for dinner.

She goes back to her book. I pull the quilt tighter around me and imagine it's Will.

Everything in my head is churning and flitting. I can hear my heart beating, my thoughts racing around like the gulls. *Will's hands playing with the sand while we sit on the shore and talk about books. Beth in the rain telling me stuff I don't want to hear. Casey going all protective. A spiral of smoke pouring out the café window from a pile of burning books.*

But this is the only place I can be right now. Granne and me, here on the deck, wine and book, and then, after the sun sets, just wine. Then tea. We're in the right place, even though I might be twitching a bit inside my smelly, sandy quilt. Granne and me, on the deck in the dark, waiting for my dad to arrive.

I think he texted from practically every rest stop and gas

station and service center along the Trans-Canada. The last one was from Sackville.

Stopped for coffee at Tim's. Will roll down windows and let you know if the piper is playing when I cross into NS.

I read it out to Granne and she smiles at that one.

"An hour away. He'll be tired, so that coffee will help." I think she's reassuring me, but it's possible she's reassuring herself. "And the piper will not be playing at this time of night." But she gives me a raised-eyebrow look as she says it. *Oh, Andrew!*

I maybe doze a little. I'm tired—so tired after the past few days of revelations and scares and questions. Even with that long sleep Wednesday into Thursday. Today, Friday, was all about cleaning and organizing the café for Monday's delivery of furniture and appliances. Billy was there briefly, quiet and closed-off as he checked measurements and finished some small adjustments to the countertops, the drawers, and cupboards in the kitchen. He and Granne didn't talk much and I hid inside myself with the books, hoping Will might show up, too. Knowing he wouldn't. The shelves are all full now, and the few remaining boxes are stacked under the table in the storage room.

Billy left mid-afternoon and Granne and I headed home shortly afterward, to supper, and the deck, and watching the tide come in, and pushing away everything else to wait for my dad.

And then, finally, there's a light down the road. I was dozing but I'm awake now. It's him, I know it. I stand up, still wrapped in the quilt, to watch the cloud of light in the distance become· headlights, become a dark machine booking it toward us down the road, become the hum of engine and tires, become the familiar suv crunching in over the stones of the driveway and stopping. The sound of waves down on the shore returns as he shuts it all off, and then the door opens.

Flinging off the quilt, I'm down the stairs of the deck before he can even close the car door, and he's ready for me, arms open wide.

#  Ready

"Nice, Mom. Wow. Really nice."

Dad stands in the main room of the café, revolving, exactly the way I did that first day, when it was just a construction zone and I freaked out. He's not freaking out. He's smiling a Christmas morning kind of smile. He looks at Granne, and I can tell she's trying not to show how much she loves that he loves this place already, even without tables, chairs, and a place to cook a grilled cheese sandwich.

It's Monday. We spent a rainy weekend not doing much of anything because Dad was exhausted. I could see it in his face, hear it in his voice that first night as we stayed up well past midnight, sitting on the deck in the dark, catching up. I'm not sure Dad and Granne slept at all that night because I could still hear their murmuring voices on the deck after I said goodnight and stumbled off to bed. Tired, but not empty. Not at all.

Dad was full of coffee. I was full of Dad. Having him sitting there next to me on the deck with his legs stretched out and a can of beer in his hand and his head resting, tilted up, against the chair back so he could look at the stars—I hugged the quilt around me as he talked and talked. About Mom, and the doctors, and the place she's staying now, with people watching over her. About my grandparents, finally getting the picture that it isn't anything they can fix, and how sad they are, and how we need to go visit them at some point, but not now. Later. About closing up the house and asking that middle-school kid down the street to keep an eye on the grass. Giving an extra key to nice Mrs. Prentice next door so she can come in and make sure everything's okay, pick up the mail.

"What about Lynette?" I ask from inside my quilt cocoon.

Big sigh. "Yeah, maybe we can talk about that later," he says, and he reaches over and squeezes my knee, and that's all.

It's Granne who suggests we get off to bed, we have all weekend to catch up, all that. I'm the first one to move because, honestly, I'm so ready to crawl under the covers and disappear. But they stay out on the deck for a while longer, and I can hear the gentle hum of their voices as I slip into sleep. They're probably talking about me but I don't care. I feel as if I'm six years old, little and safe, tucked up in bed while the grownups carry the world.

So now it's Monday morning, and we're at the Tuttle Harbour Café and Reading Room, waiting for the deliveries of furniture and appliances, and Dad is acting a bit like a kid on Christmas.

"Mom, honestly, I could never have pictured this old place cleaning up so well. And the books—the shelves—Billy Greenfield, am I right?"

"Billy built the shelves and Larkin loaded them," says Granne. She's enjoying the show, I can tell. Nothing like watching your kid act like a kid, I guess.

I'm still standing by the door and he comes over to pull me in for a hug.

"Wow, Larkin. Just wow."

Pretty sure that means, *Nice job on loading the bookshelves without doing your book freak-out thing*, but I don't care. He's here and he's happy. It's just possible that right now, at this moment, I'm happy, too.

It's a crazy, busy day. Billy shows up shortly after we do, ready to unload furniture and install appliances.

"Hey, Billy, great to see you!"

Manly hugs between my dad and him, which I find astonishing. Billy actually laughs and smiles, which is also astonishing. (No sign of Will, which is not astonishing.)

"Great to see you, Andy. It's been too long."

"Way too long. How's Suzanne?"

"Keeping me in line," says Billy and he shrugs, maybe thinking about the fact that everybody is saying he got out of line. He doesn't ask about Mom.

"I'm sure I'll see her while I'm here. And Willie?" I had no idea my dad was so well-informed.

"Yup, Will's working at the Co-op this summer and helping out here," Billy says, glancing at me. "One more year at the high school, then off to university."

Dad shakes his head. Kids growing up so fast and all that. They talk some more, but I slip by them to the storage room to get out of the way. I don't want to be around while they talk about Will, or me, or possibly other family stuff. I pick up a box of already sorted books and lift them all out on the table to sort again. A make-work project.

No. It's a hiding-in-the-storage-room project.

Whatever. It's working.

"That has to be one of Becca's," I hear Dad say, and I picture them looking at the bookshelf rug, now hanging in one of the few spaces between shelves.

"Sure is. A beauty."

"Yup. A beauty."

The rug, I assume. Or could they possibly be talking about Becca?

The roaring engine and grinding brakes of a large truck can be heard outside. The appliances have arrived and, after that, it gets noisy and busy.

Becca drops in late morning and there's another reunion.

"Andy!"

"Becca, so great to see you!"

I hear laughter and picture their hugs as they meet up in the middle of the still table-less, chair-less main room. High school reunion time, obviously, as Billy peels away from helping with installation of a dishwasher in the kitchen and slips past my door to join them.

"Goodness," says Granne. "I'm having a flashback."

Granne just made a joke. What is happening?

The furniture arrives shortly after and Dad comes to find me.

"Nice little cave you've got here, Lark," he says looking around. "It's pretty noisy out there, eh?"

"Yeah, I thought I'd just stay out of the way until Granne needs me to do something." I shrug. "Me and my books."

I can see he's about to say something but he hesitates—mouth forming the words and then not saying them. He was going to say something about me and my books, I know. Instead, he suggests we head over to the bakery for a coffee run.

"I haven't had my requisite daily cinnamon bun yet. You in?"

"Sure." I know this is probably just him trying to give me a break from the bedlam going on, and I'm grateful. "Let's go."

And it is bedlam. But an exciting, good kind of bedlam. There's a huge fridge free-standing just outside the door of my little room, and Dad and I have to squeeze past it to get to the main room, where Granne and Becca are peeling plastic coverings off chairs and stacking them out of the way against one of the walls of shelves. In the open space, the furniture guys are unpacking and constructing the tables. Assembly required, apparently. Noises coming from the kitchen include electric tools and the thumping of large metal appliances being shoved, maneuvered, and scraped across the floor. Even a few swear words, followed by Billy sticking his head around the fridge, saying, "Sorry about that, Mrs. D." Granne replies without looking up from her chair duties, "No worries, Billy. Carry on."

"Coffee run," Dad calls out as he guides me toward the door and stops, with a scrap of paper and a pen. "Taking orders."

It's nuts with people calling out, but Dad gets it all down, and I picture what he must be like in front of his Grade 12 English class, or when he's directing the school play. Calm. In charge. A lot like Granne. Nothing like me.

Becca gives me a smile on the way by, two smaller rugs in her hands. "Exciting, eh?"

"Sure is." I wonder if she told anyone about me and the post office and Jonah's letter. Something tells me, no. Something tells me she's just that sort of person who doesn't share other people's secrets. So I smile at her, and I hope she knows that means, *Thank you.*

"It's good here, eh, Lark?" Dad says as we drive across town. I can see him glancing over at me, maybe looking for signs of the bruises around my eye, my jaw, now faded and gone. "You've been okay here?"

Pretty sure this is my dad feeling guilty for leaving me behind when he went to Vancouver.

"Yeah, Dad. It's good here. And yes, I'm okay."

Well, I'm okay if you don't count a couple of public meltdowns, a drunk night at the back shore, some creepy mail from back home, also a few scary suggestions from a mean girl about a boy I like—a boy who now seems to be avoiding me—and, yeah, all that. Sure, I'm okay.

"Good," he says and sounds relieved. Mission accomplished.

Good. Everything's good. Sure it is.

# What's next

"She was a mess, Lark, I'm not going to lie to you," says Dad.

I can't look at him, but I reach in and wrap my arms around him as we walk. His right arm comes around my shoulders and he wipes his eyes with his left.

Yes, my father and I are walking slowly along the shore, crying together.

"I missed you so much," I manage. "I wanted to be there."

"I know. It was just so hard, Lark. Worrying about you and what happened there at the end of the school year, and then trying to deal with John and Sylvia—you know how they are. They live in that 'everything's fine, don't show the neighbors' kind of world. It would have been really hard on you, too." He means, it would have been hard to explain the bruises, my freaked-out, frozen state of mind.

"I know." I do know. My Vancouver grandparents have never

been the warm and fuzzy types. Actually, Granne isn't warm and fuzzy, either, but somehow it's not so bad with her. Maybe it's the high school principal part of her that makes her different.

"And the whole scene with your mom was just—well, it was a shit show, if you don't mind me saying."

"I know, Dad. I get it. And, actually, I love you saying."

Okay, that makes him laugh.

"She's beyond our help now and she's not going to get better," he says after a while. "I hope you understand, Lark."

We've reached the end of the beach and stop together. The tide's going out and our path takes us deeper and deeper onto the first sandbar. Dad disentangles himself gently and reaches down to pick up some flat stones. Skims them out across the water. I wonder how many million times he's done this in his life, growing up here.

Ebbing tide. And calm tonight. Quiet, except for a few squawking herons, some piping plovers. The sun is down below the horizon, but the sky is lit up with fluorescent pinks and lilacs, streaking up to the few puffs of clouds hovering just over the water.

I can't help myself. I glance over my shoulder, just in case he's there, coming over the point.

He's not. Of course he's not.

Dad throws a few more stones and we turn and start walking back up the beach toward Granne's. This is our fifth turnaround. We've been out here since almost right after supper, which was fish and chips picked up at the roadside diner again, because Granne said she was too tired and frazzled to make anything after our day of labor.

We've covered a lot of territory, Dad and me.

"Granne says you've had a couple of episodes of anxiety."

"Yeah, I guess."

"You know, we could get you some meds. I know we talked about that back home, and you and Dr. Gaboury decided you didn't need them, but I could take you to the health center here—"

I cut him off. "No. I don't want anything. No pills."

Meds. Pills. As if I want to go down that road, like my mother and her pain turning into a black vacuum that just sucks you down. Maybe I'm exactly like her—a few pills just to help get over the trouble spots. Temporary. Just a few times, just like the booze. And then it becomes more than a few times, becomes necessary, becomes a destroyer. No, I'd rather have a freak-out in public and have Granne hold me up, or Becca.

Actually, I'd rather have Will take me kayaking with the seals.

"Okay, I get it. You're strong, Lark. I know it's been tough. I'm so proud of you."

*No, I'm not strong,* I want to tell him. I wonder if Granne has told him about that first time at the back shore, staggering home drunk. About how many hours I've spent wrapped up in my quilt in my room with the door closed. Doesn't matter now.

We talk about other stuff, too, like Lynette.

"So, she's gone then?"

"Yeah. Found a new place," he says and he sounds almost embarrassed, which is kind of sweet. Like he's my age and trying to explain his behavior to a parent. "You know, I told her things were just too uncertain for us—you and me—right now. She thought she was helping. *I* thought she was helping, you know? Just having someone, an outsider, to kind of keep things normal around the house." He shrugs. "And she is a nice person."

I glance at him. Yes, Lynette is nice, I guess. Annoying, fussy, talks too much, but whatever. I thought maybe she made him happy and kept him distracted enough not to notice I was falling. Yeah, I think she was pretty good at that. Until she had to come up with the makeup to cover my periorbital hematoma.

Then I could tell she was losing the niceness.

"Dad. Things weren't normal," I say and he looks at me, looks away.

"Yeah, I know. I knew that."

Normal. Whatever that is.

"So, speaking of normal," he says. "Grade 11 at Bayview."

"I can't go back there." The words are hardly out of his mouth before I say it. "I'm not going back. I'll do home school or online or transfer to the Catholic school or something, but I'm not going back to Bayview."

There. I say it out loud, the thing that's been crashing around inside my head—along with all that other stuff—since the last day of exams when I left the Accommodations room and walked down the hall, past all those knowing eyes, toward the nearest exit, found my way home, crawled into bed, and shook for an hour before throwing up and sneaking downstairs to steal a bottle of red from the wine rack in the basement.

I don't even tell him about Jonah's letter. I'm not sure what he can do about that, but I have a feeling he'd be on the phone in a heartbeat, long distance, to Mrs. Parker-Li, and that probably wouldn't end well, judging by the few conversations they've already had. Nope. That's my little secret—mine and Becca's.

"I'm just so tired of people talking," I say. "People are still talking about me—that's what people do. They talk and they don't always know what's going on."

"Yeah, welcome to high school. Or a small town," he says. "Like, what's this thing Becca was telling me about Billy? People actually think Billy started the fire at the café?"

"That's exactly what I mean. It's just people talking about other people."

Beth and her face close to mine in the rainy parking lot. *And apart from Will, there's his dad. Of course you know what happened with the fire at the café, right …?*

"You don't believe it?"

"No. I don't. But I think Granne does."

I tell him about Billy and Will coming over to tell her about everyone talking, about how they will stick with the job, do it right. Prove everyone wrong.

"I find it hard to believe Granne would buy into that kind of thing," he says. Shakes his head.

"I was there. I heard the conversation. It's the same stupid thing," I say, and I can't stop the angry wobble in my voice. "It's people talking. Just like school. Just like me and that stupid thing that happened."

"Okay, I get it," he says, gives me a squeeze. "Don't worry about going back to Bayview. We'll think of something."

So we walk some more, farther out on the sand. A few more flat stones. A few more herons. We talk about Mom. We cry a bit.

"So many things have gone wrong for us lately, but you coming here was a good idea, Lark," he says.

We're standing at the bottom of the rocky path that leads up to Granne's lawn, her house, where we can see her still sitting on the deck in the dusk. She's been watching over us as we walked.

"Yup," I manage, and sink into him for one last hug before heading up to join her.

"With everything that's happened, to you especially, it's good to remember that there are places like this, with good people. You have to believe in people, Lark," he says, both arms wrapped around me now and his chin resting on the top of my head. "It's a leap, maybe, and it doesn't always work out. But you have to trust people."

I understand all that. But he left a few things out, such as: You have to trust that sometimes people are going to try to hurt you.

We start up the path toward Granne, and I take another look back at the point to see if anyone is silhouetted there.

No. Just the shore birds, still wheeling around against the sky.

But that's okay because now I have a plan.

# Setup

On Tuesday night, Granne is going to Amherst to raid one of the big-box stores for bulk plates and cutlery, coffee and tea. She's having supper with one of her retired teacher friends who's offered to get the word out over there, and she's told us she won't be back until later in the evening.

And on Tuesday night, my dad has a date with Becca.

Okay, so it's not a date. They're going to Tatamagouche for chowder at this place he hasn't been for years.

"Best chowder ever, Larkin," Becca said at some point on Monday afternoon. "You should take your dad."

"Yeah, maybe," I say.

I'm thinking about something Chelsea and I talked about over our ice cream. Thinking, this could be it. "You know, I'm kind of off chowder right now." Dad gives me a look, which I ignore. "You guys go, though. I don't mind fending for myself. Go tomorrow, if you want."

They look at each other and it would almost be weird— the way they do that, as if they've just thought about going out together, like on a date—except I'm already thinking about how I can make this work and ignore the vibe they're sending out.

A brief, almost awkward silence, then Dad says, "You sure, Lark? You should come."

"No, I'm good. Actually." My brain is ticking over, thinking, thinking, making something up. "I'd kind of like to rearrange the books. I think the Kids' section should be over there, where there's a bit more space. I might mess around here for a while tomorrow and switch it with Biography. Make sure the books are all perfect."

Dad and Becca are both looking at me as if they're about to say something. Something like, *We'll wait for you.* Or, *We'll help.* Or, *No, it's fine the way it is.* But I can tell the idea of going to Tatamagouche for supper together is working, too. I milk it.

"Guys, just go. I'll get Chelsea to help me," I say. "She's finished at the bakery late afternoon and she can drive me home. Maybe we can cook up macaroni together or something."

It's a plan and it works. In all sorts of ways.

"Well, okay," says Dad. He glances at Becca and she shrugs. *Look at Larkin, taking control of things, looking after herself. And Chelsea Burgess is a good kid, no worries there.* "Okay, Lark. Is that okay with you, Becca?"

"Works for me. Chowder works for me anytime," she says and smiles at me as if I've done her a favor.

"So, you'd be all right on your own for supper tonight, then?" Dad asks as he and Becca get ready to leave late on Tuesday.

Dad, Billy, Becca, and I have spent the afternoon cleaning up the café kitchen now that everything is installed—vacuuming up the sawdust from floor and drawers, and wiping down counters. We mop the floor in the main room, dust everything, arrange the tables and chairs. Once everything is cleaned up, Billy and Becca hang a few more rugs in the spaces between shelves. Tomorrow, Granne will confirm the big order with the bakery, the supplier of muffins, cookies, and squares. That's the menu for now, although she says she wants to expand to sandwiches and soup at some point in the future. Maybe hire a chef.

"Once we see how it goes. See if anyone actually comes

through the door," she says.

We all know people are going to come through the door on Thursday. The buzz is everywhere and it's building. Someone from the local county newspaper came and interviewed Granne this morning, took a picture of her standing in front of Becca's beautiful big rug with the books. People have already been showing up at the door all day—right in the middle of our big clean—asking if we're open for business.

"Can't wait," says one older lady, who is known by everyone but me, apparently. A local. She turns up while the reporter is here. "A cup of coffee and a muffin in a room surrounded by books. I mean, does it get any better?" I can see the headline taking shape already.

"Well, that's it for me," says Billy, looking around at the job he just completed for free. "I'm off home."

"Hey, Billy," says Dad, shaking his hand longer than necessary. "Thanks, man." I think my dad wants to talk about the rumors, but Billy gathers up his tools, is already moving away, shutting the door on that conversation. He just nods, smiles that crooked smile of his, and leaves us.

There's a pause, words unspoken that I can almost hear, and

then Dad says, "Okay then, Lark. I guess Becca and I are off to do the chowder thing. You're sure you don't want to join us?"

"Yeah, I'm sure. Have fun."

"And you've got the key, right? Give everything a once-over before you leave and lock up, okay? Back door, too?"

And, after a few more parental instructions, they're off. I'm alone in the café.

It's time.

It doesn't take long. A text to Chelsea—she gave me her number the other night and this is the first text I've made on this phone to anyone other than Dad since he disappeared my old one. I know she's still on duty at the bakery for another half-hour or so, but she'll be waiting for me to let her know the coast is clear.

We're on

I spend fifteen minutes exchanging the Biography with Kids and trying to ignore the fact that my hands are shaking.

And then I wait.

# Behind closed doors

Beth shows up at the door just as Chelsea and I are finishing off our supper of the day's leftover ham and cheddar sandwiches from the bakery. Also, cookies.

I can hardly eat, but Chelsea rips into hers with gusto and then follows up by downing the half-sandwich that I can't manage. What is it about skinny people being like birds, being able to eat a lot and burn it off immediately? It's not fair.

"Hi, guys." Beth appears at the door, and we didn't even hear her footsteps on the verandah. Yup. Just like a cat.

"Hey, come on in," says Chelsea just as I come in from the kitchen where I've been standing, staring out the back door, and fighting the urge to go hide in the storage room. "We're just bingeing on bakery leftovers, then I can give you a lift home."

"Hi." I smile as normally as I can manage. After all, smiling has not really been in my vocabulary of facial expressions recently. And let's face it—the last conversation between Beth and me wasn't exactly warm and fuzzy.

"Okay. Thanks for the lift, Chels. Anything for me?" She doesn't even look at me but reaches for one of the cookies Chelsea points to. "Crap day at the office. I could use some sugar."

"Yeah, the bakery was nuts today, too," says Chelsea.

"It was pretty nuts in here today, too," I manage to join in. "Getting everything ready."

Beth munches and looks around. Nods without much interest. I see her eyes rest on the kitchen with its shiny new appliances, on the door to the storage room.

"It's cool, isn't it?" Chelsea says. "Larkin has to babysit the place while her grandmother and father are off doing last-minute errands, so I brought her some treats. Figured you might like to have a little preview, too, before I drive you home."

Chelsea is running away with this, which is great, because I'm incapable of speech and I just let her talk. Nod. Smile. Try not to vibrate.

"Yeah. It looks good," says Beth, munching. "I should get going, though, Chels. Are you nearly ready?"

"Oh, shoot," I say, out of nowhere and maybe a bit too loudly, and Beth turns to look at me. "Sorry, guys, I forgot something. My grandmother asked me to go over to the hardware store and get some more cleaning supplies. She'll be mad—sorry, I'd better get over there before she gets here. Can you just wait till I get back, so I don't have to lock up? Not let anybody in?"

"You go ahead," says Chelsea. "Be quick, though, eh? We have to get going."

"I will." She and I nod at each other and I manage to leave without glancing at Beth once.

Outside I pause, out of view of the open windows, just for a moment, and I hear Chelsea say, as we planned, "Do you think we should tell her? I mean, about Billy and the fire and everything?"

And Beth giving a short laugh. A snort, really. "No. Why would we?"

I turn and walk toward the hardware store, and I might even be smiling, because now I know.

# Over

I come back with the bag of stuff I didn't really need and they're sitting at one of the tables, demolishing the cookies. Chelsea grins at me.

"I saved one for you," she says, nodding at a chocolate chip cookie sitting on top of a crumpled and butter-soaked paper bag.

"Aw, thanks, Chels." I go into the kitchen and put my stuff down, then come back and join them. "My favorite."

A cookie never tasted so good.

"This place is really great, Larkin," Chelsea says. "It really turned out well. Your grandmother must be really happy."

"I think she's pretty excited. And speaking of Granne," I grab my phone out of my pocket and check the time. "I think she'll be back soon and it might be best if you guys cleared out before then. I mean, it's not a problem if you're here, but, you know. I'm supposed to be working and everything. Big list still to get through." I wave vaguely at the shelves as if the books need rearranging.

Beth gets to her feet and brushes the crumbs off her hands over the table. "Come on, Chels. I haven't heard from Casey today, but I bet we'll be heading to the shore for a swim."

"Sure … okay." Chelsea stands up, too, gathers up the empty bags, and scrunches them into a ball. "Thanks for the preview. I'll be here to help you with kitchen duty on Thursday night after work, right?"

"Yeah, okay," I say. "We'll be open for business during the day, and then Granne will have an official opening sometime in the evening. You know, she's got the town councilor coming to say important words. Ribbon cutting. That kind of thing."

Beth smirks. Clearly this small-town excitement strikes her as less than exciting. She's already on her way to the door. "Have fun with that. See you, Larkin."

"Okay, Bethy, let's roll." Chelsea turns to me. "So, I'll check in with you later, okay? You're good here for now?"

"Yeah, I'm good." Our eyes meet for one significant moment. "Thank you."

"Go get 'em," she grins, and she's out the door, leaving me alone.

Well … not quite.

I hear a sound behind me and he's there, just coming around the door of the storage room. He's been in there listening since he arrived earlier with Chelsea, after she called him and told him there was something he needed to hear. It was awkward when he arrived at the door of the café. I could tell he didn't want to be here, where I was. Didn't want to meet my eyes.

"Just trust us," Chelsea told him, and he shrugged and walked past me without saying anything. Shut the door behind him.

Now he's watching me, hands in the pockets of his jeans.

We don't say anything for a moment, just stand there looking at each other.

Well, one of us has to say something, so I start.

"You heard them?" I know he did. Of course he did.

He nods, takes a few steps toward me.

"Yeah, I heard them. I heard it all. She threw her cigarette in there," Will nods back at the storage room. "Came in the back when Dad was out there talking to Becca. She and Casey were going by and she saw my dad out there and wanted to stir up shit. Get back at me, maybe at you a little."

"Me? Why?"

He shrugs. "Because we were friends. Because I dumped her."

"So, you guys were … you and Beth?"

"Yeah. Me and Beth. Last year." Shrugs again, embarrassed maybe. "It wasn't anything. I don't even think she liked me that much."

But she was new at the school, and he was nice, and smart, and a good guy. And it was a way for her to get Casey's attention, too. I know girls like this. Every high school, every town, has them.

"She's a liar, Larkin. You know that, right?"

"Yeah. I know."

We stand there for a moment longer, and then he takes another few steps toward me and I feel—I feel absolutely nothing as I stand there looking at him. No fear, no anticipation. I just stand there, thinking how good he looks.

Will takes the final few steps toward me and, before I can say or do anything, he reaches out and slowly pulls me in for a big, arms-tight-around-me hug. He holds me so close I can hear his heart beating, and I don't even feel like pulling away, I'm so tired. I'm just crumpled up against him, empty.

My head is pressed into his shoulder, and his one hand holds me there, his mouth close to my ear.

"Thanks, Larkin."

# The real story

"Are you okay, Lark?" Dad asks when I emerge from my bedroom cocoon and join them in the kitchen, much later.

He and Granne are sitting at the table going over The List for the grand opening on Thursday, her wine and his beer in progress. Becca was here for a while, too—"One glass of wine, Anne, but that's it. I'm full of chowder"—so I wait until she's gone. Until it's just us, the home team.

They both look up when I come in and I think how alike they are. The straight mouth that smiles gently, lifting up just a little on both sides. The cleft chin, like mine. And those piercing blue eyes that see everything—seeing me now, with a question in them.

What they see probably isn't something great. I'm so empty and exhausted since Will dropped me off a few hours ago that I've been curled up on my bed with the quilt pulled over my head.

I hear Dad and Becca get home first, then Granne. Conversation, footsteps. My door opening and closing as someone, probably Dad, checks on me and goes back to the kitchen.

"Are you okay, Lark?"

"I'm fine, Dad. But I've got something to tell you guys."

Neither one moves, but it's easy to see they're expecting something bad. The slight tightening around the shoulders, the eyes narrowing as I drop into a chair and look away, down, at the table.

There's a pause as I try to find a way to start, and then I hear my dad sigh.

"Just out with it, Lark. What's wrong?"

That's the perfect word to get me started.

"What's wrong, is that Billy didn't start the fire at the café. It was Beth."

I look up at them then and there's a moment when they both look dazed, as if they're trying to understand what I just said. I'm pretty sure they were expecting something completely different. *I'm pregnant. I'm hearing voices in my head. I killed someone.*

"Beth McAdam? Are you sure?" Granne sits up even straighter than usual, like she's snapping to attention in her chair. On alert. "What makes you think so?"

"I know so, Granne." And so I tell them.

She listens to me as I describe the little sting operation Chelsea and I set up. How Chelsea had heard hints from Beth about what really happened on the night of the fire; how she picked up Will and convinced him to wait in the storage room; how I left them alone so that Beth would talk about things she would never talk about with me in the room. How everyone was talking, talking about Billy and the fire, and it just wasn't fair—

"I'm just so tired of people talking," I say, finally.

No, I don't say it. I'm out of air. I whisper it.

I look over at my dad, who just got back from watching Mom sink out of sight and, not long ago, had to carry me, his drunk, beat-up daughter, into an emergency room, and is probably thinking that things have just *got* to get better.

"Larkin," Dad says, reaches over and squeezes my hand.

Granne doesn't say anything, but she stands up so quickly that her chair screeches against the floor. She goes over to the phone, presses in a number.

"Suzanne? Anne Day. Is Billy there?"

## Billy

Dad and Granne are at the table, talking. I'm curled up in the rocker over in the corner, near the stove. I'm nearly finished the last of Becca's yarn, and my hands work the needles with a rhythm that feels like heartbeats.

"Are you thinking of pressing charges or anything, Mom?"

"No. None of that nonsense," Granne says. I love that she calls arson 'nonsense.' "But I do want to talk to her. Casey Henwood, too."

Did my dad just snort-laugh? I think so, and I bet I know why. Beth and Casey just got called down to the principal's office.

"The McAdams, and Clay and Cathy Henwood, too," she says. "I think that will be sufficient."

I almost smile at that. Such a teacher word: *sufficient*. When I glance at her, she's watching me.

"No need to bring the RCMP in," she says as our eyes meet

for a second. She nods and turns back to Dad. "It's done, thanks to Larkin."

I knit. I breathe.

I'm empty but, tonight, since Will whispered, "Thanks, Larkin" into my ear, it feels like a different empty. As if everything inside me has been tossed out and I'm ready to be filled up again.

I'm smiling about that image when Billy arrives.

"Billy, come on in."

Dad jumps up and slides the door open, and they nod a greeting as Billy slips into the kitchen.

"Hi, Andy." Billy looks around, at Granne, at me, still curled up in my corner with my knitting. "Hi there, Larkin. Is everything all right, Mrs. D?" He sounds nervous.

"Everything isn't all right," says Granne. "Sit. Please, Billy. I'd like to talk to you."

So he sits and I can barely look at him because he's suddenly frozen, hands clenched in his lap.

Granne sees it, too, so she smiles at him and starts to talk. About the great work he and Will have done on the café, about trusting him with the job because he is the best in town. How much she values the contribution he's made.

Billy shifts in his chair. Looks uncomfortable.

"Now, go on, Mrs. D. You know I was always going to finish this job, no matter what."

*No matter what ...*

He speaks quietly, with no smile in his voice. He's sitting there, tense and upright, at the kitchen table, thinking about escaping because he doesn't know where this is going. Forced to sit there and listen to Granne, who he knows thinks he started the fire that almost wrecked her dream. He's thinking something worse is coming, maybe ...

"I'm sorry, Billy. Sorry that I ever had a moment's doubt about that damn fire," she says, and there's a shocked silence because, wow, Mrs. Day just swore.

"Mrs. D—" he starts, but she cuts him off.

"I've just learned that Beth McAdam was responsible, so I will be shutting down this talk about the fire right away. I know you're not to blame, never were to blame, and I feel sick that I didn't do more to stop all this nonsense going on, with people accusing you. I owe you so much respect and I hope you'll accept my apology."

I'm watching the scene now, still curled up in my rocking chair. I watch Billy's face as he processes what Granne just said.

When she says Beth's name, there's a flash of recognition, maybe even something darker—but Billy doesn't do dark very well and it passes. I see the actual moment when he realizes that it's okay. It's all okay.

"Well, sure, of course I do. Apology accepted, I mean. It's nothing. Forget it." He's embarrassed but he's grinning a little, too. Relief, maybe.

"It's not nothing. It's important. I hope you and Will and Suzanne will be at the opening on Thursday night. You will come, won't you?"

"Come on, Bill," my dad says when Billy doesn't reply right away.

"Okay, yes. We'll—we'll be there, if you want us," he says at last. "And thank you."

"Good. Now, Billy, let's have a toast to old friends and better times, shall we? Andrew, get Billy a beer. Or would you prefer wine?"

Dad stands up, waiting, and there's a moment while Billy looks out the window. He glances at me, looks back at Granne, and then he says, "I think I'd prefer a good strong cup of tea, if you don't mind, Mrs. D."

A heartbeat.

"Of course, Billy."

I feel my breath return, which is a surprise, because I didn't even know I was holding it. Maybe Granne hears me, because she smiles over her shoulder at me.

"Larkin," she says, "could you put the kettle on, please?"

# The Tuttle Harbour Café and Reading Room

The place is packed. And loud.

"Your grandmother must be thrilled," Chelsea says. She has to lean toward my ear and raise her voice a little, because there's so much excited conversation going on around the room.

I look at Granne, who might be delivering a lecture to Gus LeHavre, the representative of the county council, the same council that voted to close the library a year ago. She may be happy—I know she's happy—but clearly she's not missing an opportunity to give him heck, too.

"Books and reading do matter," she said in her little speech before the ribbon cutting earlier. "We lost our library, but I want you all to think of this little space as a hub for reading. Take a book and leave a donation. Bring the book back so someone else can read it after you. This is Tuttle Harbour's book hub. Your book hub."

"Anne should go into politics," whispers Becca, standing with Dad and me.

"I know," whispers Dad. "Everyone would vote for her because they'd be afraid not to."

Now Chelsea and I watch the ebb and flow of people looking at the books, congregating around the snacks on the tables, and elbowing their way politely toward us and the coffee, tea, and lemonade. I'm on duty as a server and Chelsea has appointed herself as my assistant.

"Wonderful space."

"Thanks, girls. And you must be Larkin."

"So we can just take a book, then? And leave a donation, is that how it works?"

I answer questions, pour drinks, smile, talk, laugh with Chelsea, who knows everything about everyone and isn't afraid to share it all, some of it surprising.

"He was arrested for voyeurism. I know, eh?"

"She has the most beautiful singing voice."

"See those two? They were married. Got divorced. Got married again. How does that even happen?"

It's been an hour since the ribbon-cutting ceremony and the

room is still buzzing and loud, but it's also starting to thin out. People find Granne to congratulate her, shake her hand, tell her what a wonderful thing she's done for the town.

I'm starting to think they're not coming, but as I come out of the kitchen with another pitcher of lemonade, I hear Dad say, "Billy! What took you?" and there they are.

Will and his parents. Will in a crisp long-sleeved, collared shirt, hair combed, tidied up and almost formal. My stomach lurches. Lurches in the best possible way.

"Go talk to him," says Chelsea. "I'll watch this."

"No, I'll just wait." I don't want to leave my safe corner and face him just yet. Yes, that hug changed everything.

The three Greenfields move toward Granne, and she shakes hands with all of them. Not a hugger, my grandmother. Conversation. She asks Will something and his parents both turn to look up at him as he speaks. They all laugh and he looks my way, catches my eye.

"Hello, ladies," says Casey Henwood, swimming into position and blocking my view. "Great party. Some of us are heading to the shore after this, if you're interested. How long do you have to stay?"

I wonder if he knows that I know now. I also wonder where Beth is. But then, who cares?

He leaves soon after with his parents, who spent some time over in the Fiction section, talking to Dad and Becca, catching up, I guess. Old friends. Old neighbors from The Point. Schoolmates, maybe.

The buzz is receding and I notice there's space in the room now, space between people. It's getting quieter. Chelsea says she has to get going and we hug goodbye. I start dismantling the drinks table and, suddenly, he's there beside me.

"Here, I'll help."

"Thanks."

We're back and forth to the kitchen, carrying the urns, pitchers, cups. I load the dishwasher. He brings the empty trays back, now full of cookie crumbs. We don't talk but it's okay.

"Thanks, William." Granne is there for a moment, smiling at us both. "I'm sure Larkin appreciates the help."

"No problem, Mrs. D. And, hey, looks like it was a great night."

"Yes, it was. Thank you." She moves off to talk to two women preparing to leave.

I look over at Dad and Becca standing with Will's parents.

He's smiling, and then he turns to look down at her and she says something that makes him laugh. Eyes on each other for just a moment longer, then back to Billy and Suzanne.

"You okay?" asks Will.

Maybe he sees something in my face. Maybe I'm giving off vibes. If I am, they're good ones, I think.

"Yeah, fine. Casey says they're having a thing at the back shore. Are you going?" I don't look at him but I know he's looking at me.

"No. You?"

"No, I don't think so. I'm tired."

Silence between us as I load a few more cups and he scrunches up the parchment paper from the trays.

"Too tired for the shore?" he asks.

# On the shore

The tide has just turned and the first sandbars are emerging as I walk down the beach toward the point. The waves sound different as they leave the bars, hiss a little. It's a night sound, a sound I've come to recognize now after a month here on the shore.

I've changed out of my party clothes and into shorts and a T-shirt, a hoodie tied around my waist for when the chill rises as the sun sets.

It's setting now. Creeping toward a distant finger of land that juts out on the horizon toward the Northumberland Strait. Hazy purple and blue below the horizon. Golden, pink, and lilac above, and up into the deepening blue of the sky.

I walk along, looking out over the water. I know he's there, on the sand at the end of the beach, but I hold off looking because, well, soon enough. For now, I just walk along and look out over the water, thinking about the Island. Thinking about Seafoam.

Decide I would like to visit them both one day, but maybe in a car. We could do that, Dad and me. Maybe Granne, too. Go on a road trip across the big bridge or down the shore. Eat ice cream. Visit that sheep farm and pick up my own special yarn for my own yarn stash. Stop for chowder.

Yes, he's already there when I get to the end of the beach, legs stretched out in front of him on the sand. I spread out my familiar, now smelly, old beach quilt beside him and sit.

"What were you looking at?" he asks.

"Oh, just looking over at Prince Edward Island. Thinking about visiting someday."

I wonder if he's remembering one of our first conversations. *Sometimes I think I could just walk into the water and start swimming toward Prince Edward Island. But I would never ever get there, right?*

"Are you staying for a while longer? We could do a road trip across the bridge, if you wanted to."

"Sure. Maybe. I'd like that."

*Staying for a while longer.*

Dad and I did a lot of talking yesterday. The two of us and Granne, too, and we've come up with a plan. We're a family that needs a plan now because we've been adrift for so long.

"We—my dad and I—might actually stay on with Granne after the summer's over," I say. "My dad's going to take a leave of absence from his teaching job, help Granne with the café. And I might go to school here for a while."

I wonder what he's going to make of that. I might even be holding my breath a little.

"Won't you miss your friends back home?" he says. "I mean, Tuttle Harbour's pretty small. Probably pretty boring after Toronto. And your school back there must have a lot more going on than we do."

"No, I won't miss it."

I know he's looking at me, but my eyes are fixed on the expanse of blue that stretches between me and the Island.

"What happened, Larkin? Back there? I mean, that stuff with your mom, yeah. But there's something else, isn't there?"

The periorbital hematoma. The bruises on my arms and legs that are in full view when we go kayaking. The freaking out.

Actually, it's not that hard, once I get started. I tell him about the party and Jonah's car and what almost happened. What did happen. I tell him everyone's still talking about it. That I can't fix it, can't make people understand that it was Jonah, his hands, his body, that hurt me, not some drunken tumble out of his car onto the pavement. Well, that hurt, too, but the real story is I got myself away from a bad thing and I'm still running. Everyone's talking and everyone thinks they know what happened, and I'm too tired to even try explaining it to them. That my high school is the last place I ever want to go again. Ever.

Maybe it's true that I'm running away to Tuttle Harbour. Me and Dad both. I don't even care if Will knows, because it doesn't matter anymore.

There are only so many things you can fix. I fixed one thing, didn't I? Here in Tuttle Harbour? And look at me—sitting on the shore at sunset with a boy. That will do for now.

Long moment, as we sit there, watching the sky and water melt into each other at the horizon. A sound—maybe the cry of a heron down the shore, maybe the voices of Casey and the rest of them, doing their nightly thing at the fire.

And then Will says, "You know, I hear the high school here is pretty good."

I let out a long breath and don't say anything right away, but a smile surprises me, my lips curving up as if I don't own them.

I watch his hand with those long fingers, smoothing the sand between us, first one way, then the other. Like the waves. Like the way I've seen him slide his hand over the wood in the café kitchen, checking for slivers.

"Yeah? That's not what I heard."

He breathes out, an air laugh.

"Yeah? What have you heard?"

"That the kids at that school are real jerks. Into bad stuff. Liars. Dangerous, even."

He's silent, still working the sand. I lift my hand and lay it on top of his, and we sit like that for a heartbeat. Two heartbeats. Then he says,

"They have books there, you know. You'd have to read books."

I lean into his shoulder and look up at him. He's smiling now, tilting his head a little my way so he's looking down at me, and I can see his eyes.

"I know," I say. "But right now I'm not scared of that."

"You're not?" His breath on my forehead.

"Nope. I'm not scared of anything."

# Acknowledgments

Much of *Larkin on the Shore* was dreamed up as I walked up and down the beach at our summer house in Pugwash, Nova Scotia. So most of my research—such as finding out how the sky looked at sunset, or what the seals would do if I kayaked near them, or what it feels like to climb over sandstone boulders around to the back shore—was done over time, in person, and on location. Many of my own Nova Scotia experiences with small-town life, local history, and food found their way into the story.

To my editor Peter Carver and publisher Richard Dionne at Red Deer Press, as well as copy editor Penny Hozy, thanks to each of you for guiding this story through to publication.

I'm grateful to the Ontario Arts Council, which provided financial support during the early stages of writing this novel.

As always, I couldn't do any of this without my home team cheering me on: Dale, Elspeth and Derrick, and Tristan.

# Interview with Jean Mills

**What made you interested in telling Larkin's story?**

Years ago, a character popped into my head: a young girl who was so deeply affected by books and reading that she would cry. My original idea was to send her to a local book club, where she would overcome this "problem," helped by a cast of entertaining characters.

That story never got written but, over time, other pieces started to attach themselves to this fragile girl—bullying, the #MeToo movement, the importance of libraries in our communities, the beauty in families sticking together through adversity. Those elements eventually combined with my original character and became Larkin's journey to heal herself.

**A lot of the texture of the story comes from the setting—a small community on the Nova Scotia shore. Why was it important for you to have Larkin's story take place there?**

I set this story in a place I know well—the village of Pugwash and the surrounding region along the Northumberland Strait. It's where my husband's family comes from, and I've spent a lot of time there. It's a magical place because, as soon as you are down on the shore next to the water, with nature all around, you are changed. My time on the shore is special, maybe even healing.

That's what I wanted for Larkin. She arrives at Granne's as a traumatized, damaged, struggling teen. She has to find a way forward, and her first plan is to start walking out over the sandbars and see where she ends up (Prince Edward Island?). The shore becomes her jumping-off point—is she going to choose the oblivion of the water, or will she tie herself firmly to this healing place and her slowly improving life with Granne, her father, and Will?

**One of the challenges for a storyteller is deciding the order of events in the story. How did you decide which comes first: the party on the beach, glimpses of the disaster involving Jonah, the fire in the café, the plight of Larkin's mother, and so on?**

The story has a general timeline of events—Larkin's arrival, her job at the café, meeting people, the fire, and so on. But we see this through Larkin's eyes and, like all of us when we're telling our own stories, she doesn't necessarily reveal her experiences in order.

It was important to explain where her immediate trauma comes from early on (i.e., the incident with Jonah) because other things hang on that revelation—her bruises, her anxiety, her nervousness around Will. But the sadness associated with her mother's situation is revealed in bits and pieces. That's a deeper loss that is fundamental to Larkin's unhappiness. I wanted the reader to wait, to ask questions, to wonder about her mother's story, rather than to simply lay it out at the beginning.

Larkin's life is complicated, and I wanted the reader to experience that complexity, too.

**The power of this story depends a lot on the voice of Larkin, a girl whose mental health has been stretched to the breaking point. How did you arrive at that distinctive voice?**

I lived with Larkin in my head for a long time before I started to write her, and her voice didn't come to me right away.

I think I wrote that opening scene—where she is sitting on the shore thinking about walking out across the sandbars—five or six times, until I felt I had found the voice I wanted for her: lost in her pain ("Anything would be better than this") but also aware of the world around her and trying to stay connected ("Okay, it's salt water, so I'd probably float a bit, which would be inconvenient.").

I didn't want her to be too much the sassy, edgy heroine who is so familiar in YA fiction, but I didn't want her to be helpless and broken, either. Once the opening scene achieved that balance, I had Larkin's voice in my head and I was ready to tell the rest of the story.

**One of the issues you explore in this story is the power of gossip—"people talking"—and the way it can distort reality and cause a lot of hurt. Why was this an important theme for you to focus on?**

Social media is such a huge part of our lives now. It's the way people share stories, but it can be brutal and cruel. As a mom, a teacher, and a media professional, I've seen the power of words, online or elsewhere, to influence and hurt.

So I wanted to show how damaging "people talking" can be, not as a warning or lesson for readers, but as a reflection of real life.

I also wanted to show someone fighting back against this kind of meanness, and Larkin does that: she exposes Beth's rumors about Billy, about Will. She finally turns her back on the stories about her own false steps back home and embraces life at Granne's with her father.

**In many young adult novels, adult characters tend to remain in the background, not so essential to the plot. But in this story, there are several adult characters who influence Larkin in significant ways. Why did you choose to go against what is seen as the usual custom in young adult literature?**

I love going against "the usual custom" when I write stories and, in this case, it's easy for me, because in my experience, adults do, indeed, play a role in teenagers' lives.

Parents and other relatives, teachers, neighbors, friends' parents—maybe in fantasy worlds, the adults are missing or otherwise hold no influence but, in real life, kids interact with adults all the time. Why shouldn't that reality be reflected in YA literature, too?

**What kind of research did you need to do in order to make this a credible story?**

I follow news and media outlets closely, so I relied on my own general knowledge of current events and issues to create some of the challenges and events in Larkin's world. There were also a few trips through Google to find specific details, such as the medical term for a black eye or the traditional surnames of Cumberland County on the website of the Genealogical Association of Nova Scotia.

But most of my research was based on personal experience. As a teacher, I've helped young people navigate a wide variety of life challenges, so my research for Larkin's anxiety and distress was looking back over some of the interactions I've had.

As for researching life on the shore in Tuttle Harbour (aka, Pugwash, NS), that was just a fun dive into my own life. I have kayaked with the seals and seen porcupines and bears in close proximity, and watched countless stunning sunsets over the Northumberland Strait. A few years ago, I was introduced to the world of rug hooking and fiber art at Deanne Fitzpatrick's studio in Amherst, NS, and at the Lismore Sheep Farm in River John, NS. And nothing beats the traditional East Coast culinary treats found at the Chowder House in Tatamagouche, NS, and Sheryl's Bakery in Pugwash. (Yes, the cookies and cinnamon rolls really are magic!)

## What advice do you have for aspiring young writers who want to tell their stories?

It's pretty simple: If you want to write stories, you need to read a lot and write a lot.

The first part is easy because, if you're an aspiring writer, you probably already know how wonderful it is to immerse yourself in a book and come up for air sometime later, with the voices of those characters still echoing in your head. (Hands up if you've finished a book and immediately gone back to the first page to read it again. Yup, me, too.) You may not realize it, but you're learning how to write well by reading books that you love.

And you don't actually have to put pen to paper (or fingers to keyboard) to be writing. When you're walking to school, riding in the car, hanging out with friends—anytime you've got space in your head to think, you're giving your imagination an opportunity to work. You are writing. At some point, you do have to grab your pen or computer and actually put those words down somewhere, so developing your skill with language is important—and you're already doing that by reading (see paragraph above).

But here's my most important advice:

When my son, Tristan, was in middle school, he and I used to go to a local café, where we would drink tea and write stories on our laptops. He called it "joywriting," and I believe that joy lies at the heart of any successful writer. Write because you love it—you love the characters, the setting, the plot, the words themselves. That's where your best stories will come from, whether you share them with the world or not.

**Thank you, Jean, for all your insights.**